A ride on the wild side!

Suzanna wondered why she agreed to go on a motorcycle ride with Chase. It seemed like fun, and a little crazy. And she couldn't resist the two. Or maybe she just couldn't resist Chase Clements.

Chase straddled the big machine and revved it to life with one slash of his heel. She slid behind him as if she'd done this all her life. Her hips slid close to his, her thighs aligned with his, her belly pressed to the small of his back. The vibrations from the engine sensuously throbbed through her body.

"Hook your arms around me," he instructed above the roar.

She complied, attached her hands to the taut muscles of his stomach, pressing her pliant breasts against his strong back. He felt hard bodied, secure, invincible, and she clung to him for dear life.

"When I lean, you lean!" he yelled. "Go with me!"

"Right!" She squeezed closer to him, trying to sense his movements so she could move in rhythm with him. Being with Chase was exciting and frightening. It was the only place she wanted to be.

Although **Mary Tate Engels** has lived in Tucson, Arizona, for many years with her family, she grew up in the Deep South. She remembers it as a place where certain behavior was expected, yet every family had a rebel or two who didn't conform.

In *Hard to Resist*, Mary explores the notion that those rebels had many qualities that counted more than being conventional—as her heroine Suzanna discovers when she falls in love with Chase Clements, the town's bad boy. Mary admits that in some ways, she's one of those rebels and that's why she loves to write about them so much! In Mary's next Temptation, Chase's sister Darlene finds a rebel of her own.

Books by Mary Tate Engels

HARLEQUIN TEMPTATION

Hard to Resist

MARY TATE ENGELS

Harlequin Books

TORONTO • NEW YORK • LONDON
AMSTERDAM • PARIS • SYDNEY • HAMBURG
STOCKHOLM • ATHENS • TOKYO • MILAN

For Mama and all the "Raulston girls"
who have added such richness and fun to my life—
you'll always be young and beautiful.

Published June 1991

ISBN 0-373-25451-2

HARD TO RESIST

Prologue

SUZANNA SCHAFER'S fascination with Chase Clements began the day he saved his sister's life on Bull Shoals Lake. Before that day, he was a "troublemaker" and a "river rat." Afterward he was someone to dream about—privately of course!

Suzanna, at ten, was skinny and had straight black hair and gray eyes that were too big for her face. On that particular day, as she often did, she had set out with her father to go fishing . . .

As they walked along on the beaten path that led to the lake, he suddenly halted, lifting his hand in a sign for silence.

Suzanna skidded to a stop and listened. All she heard was the wind sighing through the pines and the high whine of cicadas that was always there on a hot summer day.

"Look here, Suz," her father said in a hushed voice. "We scared up some deer. See the signs?"

"Where?" Suzanna leaned over and studied the ground. She spotted a scattering of black pills. "Oh, that."

"Prints, too." He pointed at indentations in the soft earth. "Several kinds. They probably came to drink in the lake. This one's a doe. And another one. Over here's the buck."

"Oh, Daddy, how can you tell the difference by their feet?" Suzanna giggled.

"The buck is heavier and his toes separate, like that. The doe's print is pointed and looks solid at the top."

"Do you think they're still around here?"

"They're probably hiding nearby."

"Watching us?"

"Might be." Her father continued down the path to the water's edge, where he began to get his fishing gear in order.

"Maybe they'll come back to drink while we're here," she said hopefully.

"I doubt it, darlin'. They're scared of humans."

"Will they care if I wade where they drink?"

"No. But I want you to stay close to the shoreline. And in sight." His voice changed as he repeated a familiar warning. "Remember, there are natural holes in this lake bottom. You have to be careful."

She propped her fists on her hips and sighed heavily. "You say that every time, Daddy."

He winked at her and grinned, making crinkles at the corners of his gray eyes. Beautiful gray eyes that matched hers. "That's the way Daddies are, darlin'. Don't want to lose you in one of those holes."

"Oh, Daddy—"

"You mind me, Suzanna. Or you'll be sorry." Wearing rubber hip boots, he moved into the water.

Suzanna scanned the countryside beyond the shoreline, hoping the deer would return. She watched her father slowly maneuvering toward his favorite fishing hole, casting as he went. She had been wading only a few minutes when she heard a noise. *The deer!* she thought.

But it wasn't a deer. Suzanna looked up to see a girl, several years younger than herself, standing on the bank. She had stringy blond hair but her brown eyes were pretty. She was dressed in baggy shorts and a boy's T-shirt with racing cars on the front. Suzanna remembered her brother, Butch, had a shirt like that. But she wouldn't dream of wearing it.

The girl kicked a clump of dirt into the water. "Hey."

"Hi. I'm Suzanna Schafer. What's your name?"

"Darlene."

"Where did you come from?"

"I live right over there." Darlene pointed. "On the river."

"Oh." Suzanna realized that Darlene must be one of the Clements. "River rats," folks called them, because they lived in a shack along the river.

"Whatcha doing?"

"Looking for tadpoles. While my daddy fishes."

"I'll help you look for tadpoles." Darlene plunged into the shallows and joined Suzanna in her search.

"I thought you were the deer coming back to drink in the lake. Daddy and I saw signs of them by the path."

"I've seen deer drinking here," Darlene bragged. "I've even seen them at the river from my bedroom window."

Suzanna was immediately jealous of her—Darlene could watch *deer* from her bedroom window, for as long as she wanted to.

They waded along the water's edge, exchanging bits of information about themselves. Suzanna admired the boldness with which Darlene waded farther and farther from the shore. Apparently no one bothered *her* with repeated warnings about holes in the lake bottom. And she should know what the place was like, since she lived near here. She probably waded this lake every day.

Suzanna moved farther out from the shore, too. As the water crept up past her knees, she decided this was much more interesting than staying in the ankle-deep shallows.

Suddenly the quietness was disturbed by the sound of Darlene's name being bellowed from the pines. Darlene made a face at Suzanna. "My brother, Chase."

Suzanna knew Chase Clements. He was a "river rat," and the meanest boy in her class. He was always picking fights at recess.

"Darlene . . . Darlene!" The calling and the brother grew closer. "Dar-leeen!"

Finally, when Chase came into view and could see Darlene, she answered, "Over here. I'm helping this girl look for tadpoles."

Suzanna realized that Darlene was blaming her by saying that she was "helping" hunt for tadpoles. But Chase ignored her and concentrated on Darlene.

"Get out of that water right now!" he commanded.

"Make me!" Darlene challenged.

"I will!"

Darlene began splashing through the water as she tried to hurry out of the lake before Chase got to her. Then the splashing stopped. Suzanna looked around.

Darlene had disappeared.

Then she noticed a few strands of blond hair floating along the water's surface. Darlene must have stepped into one of those holes and lost her footing!

Icy fear clutched Suzanna, and she froze. She opened her mouth to yell for help, but no sound came. She tried again. The silence was deafening—and still Darlene didn't bob up out of the water. Finally Suzanna heard herself screaming. "Daddy! Daddy!"

She could see her father making his way toward them, moving in what seemed to be slow motion. Silence pounded in her ears. Panic gripped her and made her mouth taste like metal. In the crystal-clear water, she could now see Darlene floating just below the surface. A few pale wisps of hair remained above the waterline.

Suddenly Chase came up from behind Suzanna and jumped into the water with a splash. In one swift motion, he reached out and grasped Darlene, lifting her up out of the water. Her face looked petrified, and immediately she began coughing and sputtering and gasping for air. Chase quickly hauled her to shore on his hip. As soon as Darlene could get her breath, she started flailing her arms at her brother.

"Dumb kid!" Chase exclaimed and held on to his little sister.

Suzanna admired the boy for taking charge so readily and so well. By then her father had reached them and they had all clambered ashore.

"You all right, son?"

"Yes, sir," Chase replied, clasping his sister's hand firmly. "Dumb kid's been told to stay out of that lake."

Her father propped his hands on his hips and gently fussed at them. "This lake is very dangerous. It has hidden holes in the bottom. Anyone could fall into one, even me. You kids stay out of here. No more wading, you understand?"

"Yessir," the three mumbled in unison. Suzanna couldn't help but think that poor Darlene—all drenched and shivering—looked like a real river rat.

"I'd better get her home," Chase said. He and Darlene took off toward the house.

Suzanna's father turned to her. He looked strange, paler than usual.

Suddenly, in spite of the heat, Suzanna started to shiver. Her father draped his arm around her shoulders. "Let's go home, Suzanna."

"But you aren't finished fishing, are you, Daddy?"

"I'm finished for today."

"Where's your fishing rod?"

"Dropped it in the lake."

"You're going to leave it there?"

"I'll get Ethan to take me out in his boat later. I'm sure we can spot it in the clear water."

"Daddy? What would have happened if Chase hadn't been there?"

"Well, if someone hadn't gotten her out in time, she would have drowned, Suzanna. That's why I'm such a stickler with you. Adults are scared of those things happening."

They walked quietly a little ways while Suzanna tried to sort out what had just happened. "Then, Chase saved her life, didn't he?"

"Yes. He reacted quickly. That was quite a brave thing to do, especially for a kid."

"I was scared, Daddy."

"Me, too, darlin'."

It was then that Suzanna began to admire Chase Clements. And that admiration stayed with her into adulthood, as clearly as did her memory of that day.

SUZANNA FIGURED that by going back, she could put the fantasies to rest for good.

Oh, she knew the risks of returning. Neither places nor people stayed the same. Memories were often distorted. And reality often shattered myths. Take Chase Clements, for instance. Since childhood, she'd been captivated by him. Then he'd been taboo, and that had made him intriguing.

In her older dreams, he'd been the bad boy and she'd been the good girl who turned him around and made him see the error of his ways. But now, at age twenty-nine, Suzanna knew that kind of thing didn't happen in real life. And it wouldn't for them. Actually, Chase had never been that bad; and she certainly had never been that good.

Now that she was an adult, nobody told her what to do. Well . . . almost nobody. There was still Mama. But what Mama didn't know wouldn't hurt her.

With the childish fervor of doing something forbidden, Suzanna drove along the dirt road that separated the Clementses' property from Old Man Rutherford's. Parking her tan Toyota in a cloud of dust, she followed the path through brown grass, each step she made taking her back in time.

When she stood on the shore of Bull Shoals Lake, a hundred different memories competed for attention.

Family picnics and Mama's chicken—the best this side of the Mississippi . . . her brother, Butch, chasing her around the lake . . . Daddy fishing while she waded in the shallows, *that day*, when Darlene almost drowned . . . clandestine meetings with Chase. . . .

Summer's dryness lingered in the air. The hardwoods, dressed in their gold and crimson autumn finery, had never been more glorious. Suzanna hugged her arms. She was glad to be back in Arkansas.

Without further hesitation, she stepped out of her gray pumps and hiked her narrow skirt to midthigh. She slid her hands under the skirt, rolled her panty hose down each leg and tossed them on her shoes. Then Suzanna stepped into the shallows along the shoreline. The icy water sent a chill through her slender body. She shivered as the lake mud oozed between her toes, loving every minute of it!

Hidden from most of the world, this was a special place to her. She became oblivious to everything—caught up in pleasurable memories of her youth.

CHASE CLEMENTS noted an unfamiliar tan Toyota parked near his property. At first, he thought someone was sneaking here to fish without a license or having paid the required fee. Anticipating a conflict of some sort or other, he headed for the lake. But the sight of a dark-haired beauty wading in the shallows with her skirt hiked to her hips pulled him up short. He'd be lenient with this particular intruder.

He propped his fishing rod against a nearby pine and advanced closer to the water's edge. Then he recognized her. Suzanna Schafer. No, she was Zack's wife by now. *Suzanna! Suzanna was back.*

Chase leaned back against a tree and enjoyed the sight of her. He tipped his straw hat up with one finger and, bending a knee, propped his foot on the trunk. An approving grin slowly spread across his face.

Suzanna's dark hair was short and loose and glistened like a wet raven in the afternoon sun. She wore a silky deep-purple blouse. The way her gray pin-striped skirt hitched to her thighs and caught on her shapely buttocks made a show he fully appreciated.

Chase rubbed his stubbly chin with the tip of one thumb. He'd heard she was coming back as Rutherford's manager. But he'd taken the news in an offhand manner, telling himself that Suzanna didn't matter to him anymore. Only what was happening to Rutherford's property mattered. And the fact that she was helping him develop it made her the enemy, too.

SUZANNA'S FEET MOVED through the mud with a soft, sucking sound. A blackbird cawed loudly as he circled her, then flew away. She took a deep breath, relishing the sights and sounds, hoping that Ross would enjoy these things, just as she had when she was his age. A noise startled her, and she looked up with alarm. There, leaning casually against a tree and watching her, was a man.

Suzanna recognized him in an instant, and her heartbeat accelerated. Chase Clements had always been a little too rough around the edges to be called handsome. But because of the strong lure of his masculinity, he'd fueled many a fantasy of hers until Zack Warner had come along.

Chase grinned and raised his hand in a casual wave. "Oh, Suzanna! I see you're back."

Suzanna gritted her teeth. She'd always hated it when the kids called her that. And now, with the disturbing presence of Chase Clements, annoying memories of her childhood began to crowd out the more pleasant ones. She stepped toward him, her feet slurping mud.

He'd seen more of her legs than she cared to show him, but it seemed foolish to dash out now and pull down her skirt. "Do you like being a voyeur?" she called.

"When you're on my property, I consider it my privilege to watch. It's been a pleasure, I might add."

"Your privilege?" She propped her fists on her hips. "You haven't changed, have you, Chase? Still as arrogant as ever."

"Oh, I don't know about that," he drawled. "Some probably think I haven't changed. But I have. Too much water over the dam to stay the same. And you, Suzanna? Have you changed in eleven years?"

"Yes. A lot."

"That's good. No one should stagnate."

"You're claiming this as your property?" She pointed in the direction of her parked car. "I came down through Rutherford's land."

"I know. The road is his. But I own the waterfront along this stretch."

Suzanna was startled by the news that Chase Clements owned anything, much less this special private place along Bull Shoals Lake. "Oh?"

He moved one hand in an arc. "All this is mine. Present company excluded, of course. Didn't you know that?" He observed with undisguised approval how nicely her legs were shaped, especially above the knees, and how well that tight pin-striped skirt fit her derriere. Up close he could see that her hair was cut slightly shorter on one side than the other. A gentle wave grazed one eyebrow. Sexy.

She shook her head. "No, I—"

"Didn't know the Clementses owned anything of value, huh?" He shifted to his feet and ambled toward her. "My old man didn't do much for us, but he did leave us this river property. Once upon a time it wasn't worth spit. Now it's worth a helluva lot to some. Like your boss."

"I didn't know this was your family's."

"Nobody did, it seems. People fished this area for years without a thought as to who owned the property."

She nodded. "My dad, for one."

"Everybody did. But a few years ago I found the deed in some old boxes I was clearing out. I filed to have it transferred to my name."

She took another few steps toward the bank and looked at him curiously. "So, what do you do with all your lakefront property?"

"I run a fishing business."

"You don't look much like a businessman," she charged with a grin.

He wore faded jeans that seemed to mold his thighs and hips. The plaid design on his shirt emphasized the breadth of his shoulders and drew bands of blue and gold across his broad chest that contrasted with the taper of his trim waist. His hair, the color of dark honey, emerged shaggily from beneath a straw hat.

Chase Clements had developed into an extremely masculine, almost handsome man. And surprisingly, he owned a business. Along with the rest of the town,

Suzanna had always thought that Chase would end up following his father's footsteps—to wrack and ruin.

"I run my business like I do everything else," he countered, with no apology in his arrogant tone. "With a slow hand and a strong grip. Doesn't take a suit and tie for that, thank goodness." He gazed at her with the most annoying grin. "To be honest, though, you don't look like a businesswoman, either."

Damn him, anyway! Suzanna started to climb clumsily out of the water and found that crawling out wasn't nearly as easy as getting in. She stumbled, and he reached out to help. His hands were warm and secure as he pulled her to the bank. The energy crackled between them when they touched.

He held on for a moment.

She stood very still in the tall brown grass, looking up into his dark eyes. The breeze pushed a clump of scratchy grass against Suzanna's bare leg, and she jumped, losing her balance. He slid one hand to her shoulder and steadied her. His hand was a solid brace, and she felt light-headed.

As her gray-blue eyes met his brown velvet gaze, her composure floundered, and she started laughing nervously. "You're right, Chase. I must look ridiculous. Frankly, I didn't expect anyone to see me wading. I feel as guilty as a kid who's been caught playing hooky by a truant officer."

"That's the first time anyone ever referred to me as any kind of law officer." He paused and smiled rakishly. "I won't tell if you don't."

"Should this be kept a secret?" She tugged her hand from his and began scooting her skirt down.

"Only you can determine that. *My* reputation isn't at stake."

"Mine is?" She lifted her chin and looked squarely at him. "I'm a little old to be worrying about that, Chase. Anyway, I have my own reputation, thank you."

"Shall we compare?" He stuffed his hands into his back pockets and stood with his feet far apart.

"Maybe some other time. I should be going."

"You don't have to leave."

"I didn't mean to trespass."

"You should know that I don't consider *you* a trespasser."

"I just came down here to see if it was still the same." She tried to fix her gaze steadily on his eyes, rather than roaming his sturdy physique. But it was nearly impossible.

"And is it the same?"

"Lots of memories here, Chase."

"A few kisses exchanged on these banks, Suz. And some clumsy fumbling." He shook his head. "Ahh, I probably shouldn't remind you of that, now that you're a married lady."

"No, I'm not."

"Divorced?"

She looked down at her bare feet, now coated with dust. "No, uh, we, uh . . . Zack and I never married."

Chase barely lifted an eyebrow. "Well, that makes things much more interesting, Suzanna."

She tucked a strand of hair behind one ear. It was unnerving how his touch had lingered with her. She tried to ignore the tingles that ran all the way to her fingertips. "I'll be working nearby, you know."

"At Rutherford's?" His expression hardened. "So I heard."

"Yes. I'll be the new manager of Rutherford Country Club. I just finished talking over some details of the job with Mr. Rutherford—I have to remember to call him *Mister* now. No more 'Old Man Rutherford.'"

"Never thought you'd be working for him some-day," Chase admitted.

"Me either. Anyway, he wanted me to drive around the entire property and inspect it. He didn't say which part belonged to you."

Chase took a deep breath. "Well, I suppose congrat-ulations are in order, Suzanna. You managed to snag one of the prime jobs in the county. There aren't many of those around here. Now that you're back, maybe it'll be just like the old days."

"Not exactly. As you said, there's been lots of water over the dam. I have a son."

"A son?" Chase was somewhat startled by the news that Suzanna had an illegitimate child. Who was he to judge? Like the rest of the town, he assumed that she and Zack Warner had eventually married. "How old is the boy?"

"Ross is nine."

"Just a couple of years younger than mine."

She sucked in her breath. "*You* have a son?"

"I do now. Ken was never a secret."

"Oh, you mean Darlene's child?"

"Yep. Darlene was just a kid herself when she had him. So, Mama took him to raise. And when she died, I decided to finish the job."

"Where's Darlene?"

He shrugged. "She took off. Who knows? But it doesn't matter. Ken's a Clements. And he's mine."

"Like all this land?"

His gaze hardened. "Kind of."

"That's an admirable thing you're doing, Chase, raising Darlene's son."

"According to some, it's about the only admirable thing I've ever done." He gazed thoughtfully at the tree line, then back to her. "They might be right."

Everything about Chase fascinated Suzanna. Unfortunately, she had been so mesmerized that she hadn't even noticed the low rumblings from the sky until it was too late.

Suddenly a clap of thunder rocked the ground, followed by a gust of cool air. "It's going to rain! I've really got to go."

"We need it desperately. Been dry as a bone the last few weeks." A large drop of water hit Chase's shoulder. "It's coming fast."

"Oh, no!" she wailed. "My new shoes! If they get wet, they'll be ruined!" Frantically she searched for the place in the grass where she'd left them. Raindrops were beginning to spot her purple blouse. "Where are they?"

Chase helped her look through the high weeds. Finally he yelled, "Here!"

Suzanna scrambled toward him, reaching for the gray pumps. She could feel water trickling down her scalp.

"We're not going to make it." He hunched his shoulders against the rain. Somehow he'd lost his hat and his hair was already plastered to his head. "I know of a shelter close by. Come with me."

Without hesitation, she followed him into a thicket of pines. The fragrance of wet pine needles scented the air and, along with an urgent desire to get out of the rain, she felt exhilaration.

Chase dashed toward a small structure resembling a tree house tucked into the branches of a huge pine tree. "Deer blind...has a roof." He led the way, climbing the crude ladder, hand over hand. Then he reached down and helped Suzanna up to the makeshift shelter.

The tiny enclosure had partial walls and a tin roof that rattled noisily with the rain. Laughing and breathless, they scrambled inside and sat, leaning against opposite walls. Both were soaking wet.

Suzanna's dark hair clung to her head like a sleek swimmer's cap. She ran her fingers through it. "This isn't exactly the Ritz, but at least we saved my shoes." She looked down at her muddy bare feet, stretched out in front of them, and laughed aloud. Her crimson-painted toenails stood out boldly.

Oh, how she remembered his off-center grin. Right now, with his hair curled rakishly over his forehead, she found him as much of a hellion as he always had been.

Chase lifted one hand, opened it, and let the legs of her stylishly dark panty hose dangle. "I saved these, too."

She wanted to snatch them from him but restrained herself. "Need a souvenir of today, Chase?"

"Naw," he drawled. "My memory will do the trick."

"Good." She grabbed the panty hose from his loose grip and stuffed them into her skirt pocket. "Because I need these for work. And I might not be back."

He leaned his head back on the wall and chuckled to himself as he spoke to her. "Oh, you'll be back, Suzanna. You can't resist—"

His manner was infuriating, and she was suddenly angry at him—and at herself for the knot of tension in her stomach. She was just gullible enough to fall for his old tricks again.

He lifted a hand as if to quiet her. "You didn't let me finish."

"I can guess what you were about to say." She tried not to notice his sexy body, now clearly outlined by his clinging-wet clothes.

He sat with one tight-jeans-clad leg drawn up and his hand resting casually on his upper thigh near his crotch.

"No, you can't."

"Okay, what?"

His expression was smug. He knew he had her. "I was going to say you can't resist returning to this little corner of your childhood where your daddy fished and you waded. And I want you to feel free to come back anytime."

She sniffed and looked away. "If I have time, I might. I expect to be busy, though."

He watched her for a few moments, his thoughts anything but innocent. Well, she was damn sexy with that wet purple blouse molding to the curves of her breasts. He could even see her nipples as they responded to the sudden coolness. "I used to dream about you, Suzanna."

"Huh?" His confession startled her.

"I had never seen eyes like yours. They're the color of wild wood iris . . . a kind of frosty blue." He didn't even try to hide his blatant attraction to her.

Suzanna was stunned by his intimate admission. *He dreamed of her?* "I, uh . . ." She felt strangely heated. "I never thought about their color. I always thought they were just plain gray."

"Ahh, you've never been 'just plain' anything, Suzanna."

"I didn't think you ever gave me a second thought, Chase. We were always so different."

"We were from different worlds. Still are."

She started to deny it, but he continued. "I remember you as a rowdy little tomboy, fighting classroom bullies in the third grade."

"I always had a thing for the underdog." She grinned. "Remember when I fought big Bo Williams for teasing Mary Beth Hastings about her red hair until she cried? I got a bloody lip, and you finished the job for me."

"I didn't care a whit about the underdog. I did it because I had a crush on you."

"Chase! I never knew that."

"Oh, I kept it well hidden. But it didn't last long. I think you even fought me later that year. After that, I had a different opinion of 'that black-haired Suzanna.'"

She laughed. "I think we both landed in the principal's office more than once that year."

He shifted and hooked one arm around his bent knee. His hand was large, and prominent veins branched across the tanned top. A hardworking hand.

"At fourteen you had the longest legs of anyone I'd ever seen. I remember you beating everyone on our junior-high track team." He gave her legs an appreciative glance. "I see they're still long."

"I felt so awkward in those days," she admitted with a grin. "Taller than everyone—everyone in the world, I thought."

"At sixteen you turned into a woman, while the rest of us were still praying our pimples would go away. And at eighteen, just when I was beginning to feel confident with my new body, you ran away with Zack Warner." He paused and let the experience bring back memories. "While the rest of us wondered what you saw in him."

"Change," she answered readily. "I thought Zack would take me to all the places I'd ever wanted to see. He did, and for a while it was wonderful."

"What made you decide to return to Grace?"

"I felt it was time to put down some roots. And I couldn't think of a better place than my old hometown. I've never been to a finer place, and Lord knows, we tried them all."

"Moved around a lot, huh?"

"Zack couldn't settle down to one job or one town." She sighed. "And I'll admit I followed him eagerly. I didn't want to be condemned to live in one place. In the beginning, life with him was one adventure after the other. But after a while, all that lost its appeal. And Zack didn't uphold his end of the bargain."

"You mean he promised marriage? Did you fall for that old line?"

"Yeah, I sure did. Stupid of me, huh?"

"Well..."

"I didn't care before Ross came along. But he's in the fourth grade and has attended five elementary schools, all the way from Florida to Louisiana and up to Missouri." She shook her head and the wave above her left eye waggled. The curl had tightened in the humid air. "That's too much for any kid. And then, when my dad passed away, I realized how much I missed this place."

"Sometimes it takes a trauma to make things clear in our minds," he said in a low tone. "I never got a chance to tell you, Suzanna, but I'm really sorry about your dad's passing. He was one fine man, which isn't news to you. But something you don't know is that he was one of the few men in town to give me the time of day."

"Why, thank you, Chase. That means a lot to me." She smiled and reassessed him—again. Maybe he wasn't so bad, after all. As the cold rain splattered outside, she felt secure huddled inside the shelter with Chase. It was intimate. And she liked that feeling.

"Do you remember the day you saved Darlene's life?"

"That time you two were wading and she stepped in the hole? Of course. That was the first time I ever really noticed you as a girl who interested me."

She smiled shyly. "It was the first time I'd ever seen a heroic act, and I admired you after that."

"Wasn't very heroic . . . grabbing her the way I did, and telling her off, too."

"I was scared."

Chase laughed. "Me, too. I kept thinking that if I let my stupid sister drown, my old man would beat me within an inch of my life."

"Would he have?"

"You bet."

"But it wouldn't have been your fault."

"He didn't consider 'fault' before a beating."

Suzanna shuddered, thinking that it must have been a horrible way for a kid to live. But she never figured he had an easy life on the river. "All things considered, you've done well for yourself, Chase. Better than—"

"Better than you thought I'd do?" he muttered sarcastically. "Hell, I'll admit my family was nothing to brag about, but I've worked hard to do better. My old man, the town drunk. Me, doing everything I could get away with. Darlene, barely a teenager and having a baby out of wedlock. Mama, going against social custom to keep it."

"But she did the right thing, Chase."

"Yes, she did."

"And so did you, Chase." Impulsively, Suzanna reached out and pressed her hand on top of his. Warmth surged between them, and she felt his response like electricity through a wire.

"Every time I look at that kid, I'm grateful to Mama for not letting him go." His voice was tight. "And I have absolutely no regrets about my decision to keep him. I know that's one time I didn't make a mistake."

"I feel the same way about bringing Ross back here."

"That must have been a hard decision to make, knowing how judgmental this town can be."

"It took me a long time. But I'm convinced that in the long run, it's in his best interests."

Chase turned his hand over and let his fingers curl around her wrist. "Still defying convention, aren't you, Suzanna?"

"I'm trying to fit in. Honestly, I am."

"Is it that important to you? Fitting in?"

"Yes. It is now."

"Hope it works for you, then."

"It will. I'll make it."

He raised one eyebrow. "So you'll be staying in Grace? Even if . . ." He hesitated and looked sharply at her. "Even if Zack comes back into town and promises you the moon if you'll follow him?"

They both knew that was what had happened before.

She shook her head. "Seems like I've followed him everywhere already." She shrugged. "My future, and my son's, is here."

"Good." Not knowing why he'd said that, he went silent. What difference did it make to him where she went? Or if she stayed in Grace?

"Listen." She crawled to her knees and peered outside. "It's stopped raining. I'd better go."

They scrambled down from the deer blind. The air was damp and fresh. She took a deep breath as they walked to her car. "Ahh, I've really missed this. Missed being here."

Chase walked beside her, feeling oddly elated to be with her again. And although he'd known her all his life, he had the distinct feeling that this was a new Suzanna.

"I'll be seeing you, Chase. Thanks for the shelter." She smiled up at him. "I've enjoyed this . . . uh, meeting you again."

"Anytime you want to go wading, please feel free to come on over, Suzanna. Or if you need anything, like a friend to talk to . . ." He shrugged. "I'll be here."

"Thanks." Now she felt reluctant to go. She tossed her shoes into the car and started to get in.

"Suzanna?"

"Yes?"

"Bring your son next time you come. Ken and I would like to meet him."

"I might drop by sometime," she promised vaguely. "See ya." Suzanna climbed into the Toyota and drove away, still barefoot and soaked to the skin. But she didn't even notice her physical discomfort because her mind was on Chase Clements.

Chase waved at her car as it fishtailed through the fresh mud on the unpaved road. Suzanna Schafer had returned to Grace as a strong woman. She was a single mother who took her parenting responsibilities seriously. But she was still the rebel. She had spirit and fire, and he liked those qualities in a woman.

When she turned those eyes on him, he felt as if he'd been jabbed in the stomach. Maybe he should keep his distance from her.

Even as he thought it, he knew it would be impossible to stay away from her. He'd see her again if he had to slip onto Rutherford's property to do it.

SUZANNA DROVE BACK to her mother's, where she and Ross were staying until they could move into the small cottage that Rutherford was providing to sweeten the job deal. For Suzanna, the offer of free living quarters made the position very appealing. Otherwise, it would have been impossible for her to move back now. Job opportunities for women in Grace were scarce.

It occurred to her that they would be living close to Chase. *Very* close.

As she drove along, she couldn't get him out of her mind. She could still see him sitting in that deer blind with his wet hair curled around his head and his damp clothes molded to his lean body. And the way those eyes stared at her—

This had to stop!

She knew he could be ruthless—someone to watch out for. Messing around with Chase Clements was like playing with fire. And she had no desire to get burned again.

Well, she wouldn't go telling anyone she'd just spent a thunderstorm cooped up with Chase Clements in his deer blind. But it was an experience she wouldn't soon forget, nor would it dispel her long-held fantasies.

2

"HOW WAS YOUR FIRST DAY of school, Ross?"

"It was okay, Gramma."

"Do you know your mother went to that school? And your Uncle Butch." Ellie Schafer stood in the kitchen with a skillet in her hand. "How about eggs and bacon for breakfast, Ross? And cinnamon toast?"

Ross blinked at his grandmother. With a desperate look in his eyes, he sought his mother who sat across the table.

Suzanna nodded encouragingly. *Say yes.*

He frowned and shook his head. *No way!* "No thanks, Gramma. Cereal's fine."

"Oh, cereal's not enough for a growing boy." Ellie turned to Suzanna. "What about you, honey? You need a good breakfast before going to work."

Suzanna gestured to her cup of coffee. "Nothing now, Mama. Later I'll get some fruit or a bowl of cereal." Ellie meant well, but she was smothering them both. Well, they'd be moving to the cottage this weekend.

"Me, too, Gramma."

"Why, I always fixed eggs and bacon for your Uncle Butch when he was going to school," Ellie said in her thick-as-molasses Southern dialect. "It's hearty food for a growing boy."

"What did you fix for my mom?"

Suzanna ducked her head behind her newspaper as her precocious son took on his grandmother—using her own logic.

"Your mother was always picky." Ellie's voice lowered to a near mumble as she recognized Ross's tactic. "She didn't eat much in the mornings."

"I guess I'm like her," Ross said happily. "Thanks anyway, but I prefer cereal."

Ellie turned to Suzanna again. "Is that healthy enough for a nine-year-old?"

"We usually do more on weekends, Mama. Then we both have more time to get hungry and fix a big breakfast. And I give him vitamins every day."

"Well, that's good. I guess you know how to take care of your own son." Ellie put the skillet away, her sigh so audible no one could miss it.

"Let me see what kind of cereal you have, Gramma." Ross joined her in the kitchen and returned to the table with a cereal box and a bowl and spoon.

"Sorry, Mama." Suzanna poured more coffee into her own cup and her mother's. "I should have told you that he's picky in the mornings, too. Now, sit down and have a cup of coffee with me."

Ellie sighed and took a seat at the table opposite her daughter. She was still a pretty woman with lively blue eyes that had once sparkled with enthusiasm. But she seemed to find no joy in life since the death of her husband. Suzanna hoped that somehow her returning would help her mother. She just wasn't sure how to go about it.

Right now, all she wanted was to get settled into a place of their own. Mama had agreed to keep Ross in the afternoons after school, but they would be living independently of her. Suzanna hoped that arrangement would provide the best of two worlds. "Mama, I have an appointment with a wholesaler at the clubhouse this afternoon. I know you have your Wednesday meeting with the Crazy Quilters, so I'll pick Ross up after school."

"I don't *have* to go to the quilting, Suzanna." Ellie tucked a strand of gray hair into the tight bun on her neck. "I'll be glad to cancel for my grandson."

"Absolutely not," Suzanna said firmly. "You are not to give up your activities for us. Anyway, I want Ross to see where I'm working and where we'll be living soon."

"But you don't want him to be a bother at your business."

"He won't be a bother. Ross knows how to entertain himself while I'm doing business. When I was a waitress, then later in training for the manager's job in Lafayette, I worked early-morning breakfast groups and late-night conventions. Often I brought Ross along because I had no one else to keep him at those hours. He would either sleep or play in the kitchen or employees' lounge where I could keep an eye on him. So, we're perfectly comfortable with this arrangement. Anyway, I'm sure Mr. Rutherford and Alec will understand about my bringing him."

"Alec? You have business with Alec McNeil?"

"We're going to try to work out a deal so that his wholesale packing company supplies the club's meat."

"Oh, that's good. Very good." Ellie leaned forward on the table. "Alec's a real fine fellow, plus he's good-looking. Got lots of money. And he's recently divorced. A fine catch, that one is!"

"I'm sure. But all I want is—"

"Besides the packing house, he owns the local meat market. He pays someone else to run it for him. Drives a brand-new Chevrolet. They say he paid cash for it. I'm not surprised, because he's very thrifty." Ellie gave her daughter a knowing smile as if these were the very attributes that should make Suzanna sit up and take notice of Alec.

"I'm not interested, Mama," Suzanna said firmly. She could see through her mother's tactics and it wouldn't work. The last thing Suzanna needed was another man. Unfortunately, men described as "a catch" didn't interest her. Men more on the wild side, like Chase Clements, captured her imagination. That had always been her problem. You'd think she would have learned her lesson with Zack.

"Now, Suzanna, don't close your mind until you've met Alec. He's a man now, not a schoolboy. Anyway, you need to renew old acquaintances and make friends around here again."

"I appreciate your concern, Mama. And I don't intend to be a hermit. It's just that I have so much to do with moving in, helping Ross adjust, and getting established at work that right now isn't the time to get involved with anyone."

"I agree." Ellie folded her hands on the table.

"Good." Suzanna felt relieved to have reached some understanding with her mother.

"Sugar, I just want you to be happy, that's all."

"Happily *married?*" Suzanna shook her head. "*Please,* Mama."

"It's time you got on with your life. You're almost thirty."

"I *am* getting on with it. Working is a necessary beginning, don't you think?" To reassure her mother, she added, "Actually I've already started reacquainting myself with old friends. I ran into Chase Clements the other day."

Ellie stiffened and sat upright. "He's not an old friend."

"Well . . . yes, he is. We went to school together. I understand he's got a business now."

"The Boon Docks," Ellie said with a scowl.

"The Boon Docks?" Ross asked, suddenly interested in the conversation between his mother and grandmother. "That's where my new friend has a worm farm. He says I can come dig in it someday."

"Worm farm?" Suzanna laughed. "What's that?"

"He grows worms," Ross explained with a grin. "And he sells them to the fishermen who come to rent his dad's fishing equipment. His dad lets him keep all the money, too."

Ellie cleared her throat and cast a warning glance at Suzanna. "Sounds like that Clements kid to me."

"His name's Ken," Ross said. "And he lives right down there on the river. Wouldn't that be neat to live so close to the river? You could just walk outside and fish from your porch or swim or do anything you wanted!"

"Sounds like fun," Suzanna agreed. "But it also sounds like he works pretty hard digging those worms." Ken must be Darlene's son, the one Chase was raising as his own.

"He invited me to come over this weekend after we move. It's right next door to where we'll be living, Mom."

Ellie shook her head, then said, "Ross, honey, maybe it isn't such a good idea to go over there yet."

"Why not?"

"Well, because—"

"We don't know them," Suzanna answered quickly, backing up her mother. "Or anything about them."

"I do. He was friendly to me at school." Ross folded his arms. "Anyway, I'll bet Gramma knows him."

"Yes, the Clementses are familiar to everyone around here." Ellie arched her eyebrows. "And they aren't the type of folks I want my grandson playing with."

Ross persisted. "Why not?"

"Well, just because...their reputation isn't the best."

Suddenly Suzanna remembered Chase teasing her about ruining her reputation if she spent much time with him. And she'd countered with an ironic remark about her own "tarnished reputation." Now, here she was practicing what she'd just mocked in her talk with Chase—and worse, with her own son.

"Mama—"

"I don't care about their reputation!" Ross said angrily, pushing himself up from the table. "I don't care what you say. I'm going over there this weekend!"

"Cool down, Ross," Suzanna warned gently. "We'll talk about it later."

"No! You'll only tell me I can't go see my new friend! So why did we come to this crummy place, if you won't let me have my own friends?" He dashed from the kitchen and slammed the door to his room.

Suzanna took a deep breath. This unpleasant scene was a commonplace of small-town living. Everyone knew everyone else's business and had something to say about it. Grandmothers were often involved in the discipline of grandsons, and mothers were often caught in the middle.

"Well, that settles that," Ellie said with a hurt expression.

"No, Mama, it isn't settled. I'll handle it later, after he calms down. I'm sure he didn't mean any of it. He's angry. It's been a tough week. Moving isn't easy for a nine-year-old, you know."

"I wouldn't know about that," Ellie responded. "Because we never moved. But I can't tell you how glad I am to have you two back, even if Ross isn't happy to be here. It's been so lonesome without you."

"I'm glad to be back. So is Ross. He's simply upset now."

After Ross left for school, Suzanna began to help Ellie wash the dishes before getting ready for work. "Sounds like the Clementses are a touchy subject. What's going on, Mama?"

"Oh, that Chase has just become so high 'n' mighty since he found out he owned the land along the river. *If* he really owns it. There's still doubt among some circles. I can tell you right now, Mr. Rutherford doesn't cotton to his neighbor at the Boon Docks!"

"The feelings are mutual, I'm sure. But that's nothing new, Mama."

"What's new is Chase Clements running that fishing business."

"I think it's great that he's become an entrepreneur." Suzanna found herself defending a man she hardly knew. But it just made sense. She couldn't help feeling that the man she'd encountered in the deer blind the other day was worthy of defense.

"Well, you'd better hold back your opinions about Mr. Clements's business dealings if you want to keep your job. It's a well-known fact that your boss doesn't get along with him. I'll bet that Chase Clements would love to see Mr. Rutherford's project fold before it gets started. In fact—" she leaned closer "—Chase tried to buy the entire estate last year when he learned about the plans for the country club. Why, that land's been in the Rutherford family for nigh onto eighty years! And when Mr. Rutherford wouldn't sell, Chase was furious. No telling what scheme he's planning now."

"Oh, Mama, I can't believe Chase would do anything drastic. He's just a businessman, that's all."

"Why, he even threatened Mr. Rutherford."

"Threatened? How?"

"I don't know exactly, but I heard it was a threat, just the same. You never know with those Clementses."

"That sounds like a groundless rumor to me."

"You listen to me, young lady." Ellie wagged her finger. "Stay away from him if you know what's good for you. He's dangerous. And keep Ross away from that Darlene's kid."

"Thanks for the advice, but I can handle myself. And my son." Suzanna refused to believe Chase would do anything to prevent the country club's completion.

After her mother left the room, she wiped the table, recalling that time in the deer blind with Chase. He'd seemed so sincere, so direct. Their conversation had been honest and warm. He'd listened to her and responded sympathetically—even said something kind about her late father.

Suzanna had been surprised but impressed by what she'd learned about Chase. He had exhibited deep feelings about his family and Darlene's boy, whom he treated like a son. He had improved his life.

But, if what her mother said was true, she'd been a fool to think Chase Clements was any different. He was a hellion; had always been a hellion; and, by all odds, would always be one.

Whatever made her think he wanted anything good for her? According to Mama, he wanted the country club—and her job—to fail. What would she do if that happened? She hung the dishcloth on the rack by the sink. Her main concern was her career, and any thoughts of Chase Clements would have to come later.

When she picked Ross up after school that afternoon, Suzanna broached the sensitive subject of the Clements family right away. "I'd like to talk to you about what happened this morning."

"What?" Ross's brooding eyes showed that he knew exactly what she was talking about and that he was still angry.

"About the boy with the worm farm."

Ross kept his gaze riveted straight ahead. His facial expressions often reminded Suzanna of Zack—especially now, with his lips pressed tight and his chin jutted. His blond hair and blue eyes made her son look more like Zack than her.

"Look, Ross, I didn't mean to criticize your new friend."

He was quiet for a moment, then said in a low voice, "I guess I shouldn't have stormed out like that. But you and Gramma just made me so mad."

"I could tell."

"You don't even know Ken, Mom. He's real neat."

"You're right. I don't know him. But I know his father."

"Well, I can't help it if you don't get along with his father."

"I didn't say that."

"Then, what's wrong with him?"

She was taken aback when Ross drove straight to the heart of the problem. "I don't know. Maybe nothing. Maybe . . . you're right. We should give him a chance, no matter what has happened between his father and me."

"Does that mean you'll take me over there this weekend?"

"Well, we're moving Saturday. But, perhaps Sunday afternoon, when we've gotten settled and organized, we could go for a little while." Suzanna turned sideways to look at him. "Just to see what it's like there and to visit your friend. No one will need to know. It'll be our little secret. Okay?"

"Especially not Gramma."

She nodded and grinned at her wise son.

"All right! Great, Mom!" Ross bounced up and down on the car seat. "You're the greatest!"

Suzanna wondered if she was in fact the greatest or the dumbest as she pulled into the long clubhouse driveway. She could see Mr. Rutherford getting out of his Mercedes. What was he doing here this time of day? She'd hoped to make the business arrangement with the wholesaler alone—not with Rutherford's interference.

His large form filled the doorway, dominating the clubhouse as he obviously wanted to dominate everything, including her. But Suzanna had other ideas. After she introduced her boss and her son, she sent Ross outside to explore. "Stay in sight," she warned. "Don't go farther than the pond."

"And don't bother the ducks, young man," Rutherford admonished. "They're a mated pair from Europe. Very special."

"Mr. Rutherford," Suzanna began as soon as Ross was out of earshot, "do you have something in particular to discuss with me? You don't have a problem with me bringing Ross over here, do you?"

"Oh, no. That's okay, this time." The gray-haired man stretched to look out the window at Ross, who was running down the hill toward the duck pond.

"I'd like to tell you it won't happen again, but I can't be sure. I'm a single mother, and my son's welfare comes first. I can assure you that he won't interfere with me doing my job."

"Good. As long as you get the job done, I'll be satisfied."

"Did you have anything else?"

Rutherford checked his watch. "I just wanted to catch McNeil. What time did you say he was coming?"

Suzanna knew she had to take a stand, or she'd always have Rutherford looking over her shoulder in everything she did and every decision she made. "I was planning to meet with him myself. After all, I'll be the one placing orders and dealing with him in the future."

"I just want to make sure it goes right."

"Excuse me, sir, but I can make sure it goes right. That's what you pay me for."

"Yes, but, Suzanna, this is the first time and—"

"That's all the more reason for me to be in charge. To show everyone, especially Alec, that I can handle this job. It's very important to me, sir."

"Well, Suzanna, I'm sure you can do it."

"Then, please let me."

He looked at her for a long, quiet moment. His bushy, white-sprinkled eyebrows made a thick, furrowed line above his eyes. "I'm not accustomed to women taking charge like this. In my day, women didn't have to prove themselves."

"Only in the kitchen," she said.

There was a moment of uncomfortable silence between them. In the background, sounds of the carpenters' hammers pounded counterpoint to the beat of a loud radio. Suzanna had the feeling that her job was on the line right here, and that she had to be careful how she handled her boss. But on the other hand, if she gave in to this, he'd attend every meeting and interview she conducted. And if that happened, it was folly to think he'd sit quietly in the corner and let her make the decisions.

"Well, Mr. Rutherford," she said, "this is my day, and I can't prove myself in the kitchen. I can, however, run this country club . . . if you'll let me."

She'd made her point. Now it was up to him. Suzanna realized she was bucking the system. This was the South. She was a woman functioning in a man's world. Rutherford was the boss and not accustomed to having women taking over. This organization definitely wouldn't make the list of Best Companies for Women in the Nineties. But she had to try to make it better for herself.

They heard a truck pull up and a heavy metal door slam. Probably Alec McNeil.

"I . . . think I'll go make sure that boy of yours doesn't scare the ducks."

"Thank you, sir. You won't regret it." Suzanna watched Rutherford make his way out the back door. *Round one.* She couldn't believe she'd won. She straightened her blouse and made her way to the front door.

An antique grandfather clock, which would take its place in the clubhouse foyer when remodeling was completed, chimed four times. As Suzanna swung the door open, she felt like Scarlett O'Hara in an Arkansas *Gone with the Wind* setting. "Hello, Alec. Right on time."

The man blinked and stood stock-still. His long, thin face grew flushed as he gaped at her. "Suzanna Schafer?"

"In the flesh."

"You look different. Much prettier, er, better than I remember."

"I've cut my hair." Suzanna could barely remember Alec McNeil. He'd been a couple of grades ahead of her in school and had made no lasting impression. She gazed past his shoulder to the panel truck parked in front of the clubhouse. McNeil's Meats in bold letters decorated the side. "You've got quite a business there."

"You're still a very pretty girl."

She forced a smile. "Alec, I'm almost thirty. No longer a 'girl.' Why don't you come on into my office so we can discuss business?" She led the way past the boxed cut-glass chandeliers imported from Germany and the freshly painted Italian-made staircase to her cubbyhole office. It wasn't a bad spot for an office. Her window overlooked the golf course and the duck pond.

"This place is going to be something else!" Alex said in awe. "I've never seen inside. Like most everybody in town, I heard talk about the Rutherfords' wealth, but never seen it."

"The house is being remodeled because the Rutherford family hasn't lived here for years." Suzanna closed the door of her office and indicated that Alec have a seat. "Actually, the style is too antebellum for me, but I suppose the folks in this area will like a country club with antique furniture and Chinese rugs."

"Oh, yes, it'll be beautiful. I'm sure the new members will love it." Alec sat in one of the two Victorian high-backs Suzanna had arranged for their meeting. He was a distinguished-looking man with dark hair graying at the temples. Setting a large open-topped briefcase beside his chair, Alec propped one ankle on his knee and rested his hand on it as if he had settled in for a visit.

Suzanna cleared the end table of all but the lamp. "This isn't a very large workspace, but it'll have to do for now, Alec. Do you have that list of available products and prices we discussed on the phone?"

He paused so long before answering that she looked up, a questioning expression on her face.

"Wouldn't it be nice, Suzanna, if we got to know each other a little before we tackled the dull details of business? Got reacquainted?"

"Oh. Sure," she capitulated. She was, after all, in the South where social etiquette preceded business, and business deals were greased by social contacts. "I must have forgotten my manners. Would you like some coffee, Alec?"

"Don't mind if I do." He smiled as she crossed the room to the small drip pot in the corner.

"I've been extremely busy." Suzanna chatted as he poured two small cups of coffee. "Yesterday was my first official day on the job, and I had to start out late because of enrolling my son in school. Today I have about a million things to do, all screaming to be done first."

"You really got yourself an important job in this town, Suzanna. People are impressed."

She smiled gently as she set their coffee on the table between them. She'd been right to persuade Mr. Rutherford not to attend this meeting with Alec. Everyone was watching her, including her boss and Alec. "I think it helped that I'm originally from Grace. Mr. Rutherford preferred hiring someone who knew the area and the people."

"I think you're a smart lady, as well as pretty," he said, lifting the cup for a little sip.

Alec was being very careful not to offend her by being too forward. He was a Southern gentleman, so different from arrogant Chase Clements who implied that she couldn't stay away from him. And she could tell what Chase was thinking from the devilish gleam in his eyes. She just hoped he wouldn't be around when she took Ross to the Boon Docks on Sunday, as promised.

"My, it's good to have you back, Suzanna."

She smiled her social smile and checked her watch. "Can we get on to the business at hand, Alec? My time's running a little short."

"Sure." He fiddled in the messy briefcase by his feet and pulled out a folder. "When do you think you'll need my products?"

"Present plans are to open the restaurant just after Thanksgiving. We'll probably do some sort of promotional for joining the country club and continue through the winter with holiday and weekend meals. By spring, we hope to open the golf course and the whole place on a regular basis. By summer, it should be in full swing, with daily meals."

"Sounds like a good plan. And that'll give us time to work out suitable products and a delivery schedule."

"First, we have to decide on our menus and the type of foods we'll be serving."

"Will you specialize in Southern cooking?"

"Probably." She shrugged. "Although we haven't hired the chef, yet."

"I have an excellent supply of chickens out of Little Rock. And beef from Oklahoma. Very tender and good. Pork from upstate."

"What about fish? Could we work something out with Chase Clements? I understand he has a wholesale operation right next door. That would certainly be convenient."

"Yes, um, that's true."

"Well, what's wrong? Aren't they any good?"

"What? His fish? They're fine. And I know for a fact that he undercuts all the others' prices." Alec leaned forward. "But if I were you, I'd stay away from that place, Suzanna."

"Why?"

"Let's just say, you never know what's going on down at that river. The place seemed almost deserted for so many years, then all of a sudden, it was booming. Fast money often spells trouble. If you want any fish, let me handle it. I'll work out a good deal from someone else."

"Thanks, I'll keep that in mind." She glanced over his pricing brochure before placing it in the folder she'd prepared for his company. "Your prices seem quite reasonable. And, naturally, I'd rather deal with someone local."

"I hope you'll consider us, Suzanna. We'll deliver at any time, especially if you find that your original order wasn't enough and you need an emergency supplement."

"Thanks, Alec. I'll take all this into consideration. After I've had a chance to study these lists, I'll give you a call." She stood, indicating their meeting had ended. "It was nice seeing you again, Alec."

He pumped her hand enthusiastically. "My, my. It was certainly a pleasure seeing you again, Suzanna. And I look forward to doing business with you."

"So do I, Alec," she admitted earnestly as he clung to her hand.

He finally released his grip and lifted the messy briefcase. Pausing at the office door, he said, "Uh, Suzanna, the philharmonic is playing a week from Saturday night in Eureka Springs. Would you like to go?"

Suzanna opened her mouth to say no, but her mother's words echoed in her head. *He's such a nice man, sugar.* What harm could it do? He was a perfect gentleman. "Sounds fine, Alec."

"Great. Maybe we could have dinner before the concert? We do have to eat, you know."

She smiled weakly. "Sure."

"Okay. I'll see you later, then. And I'll call to make arrangements." He smiled happily and left before she had a chance to reconsider.

Privately, though, Suzanna was already reconsidering. With a heavy sigh, she stood at the etched-glass front door and watched Alec hop aboard the van with McNeil's Meats emblazoned on the side. She knew it was a mistake to agree to go anywhere with him. Somehow, he'd managed to get her to say yes even though she wasn't really interested in him. There'd been no sparks between them, just a comfortable feeling that she could trust him.

There was nothing to compare with the instantly flaring fire she'd felt with Chase Clements. But then, Chase had always been taboo. And apparently still was. All of which made him tremendously appealing to her.

They had clashed the minute they saw each other. Clashed, or sparked? All she knew was that when they'd been closed up together in that deer blind, she'd felt an incredible amount of electricity. When they touched, the jolt went all the way through her.

She had to stop thinking about Chase.

There were uneasy rumblings about him around town. They were short on factual truth, but she was receiving warnings just the same. She had vowed to herself to stay away from him. There was no reason to seek him out. Unless she decided to do business with him—which she was considering. Alec did say that Chase's fish prices were the cheapest in town.

But she couldn't forget the way Chase's eyes grew dark and sexy when he looked at her. His grin—that jaunty, slightly off-center crook of his mouth—was enough to drive any woman crazy for a kiss. Just thinking of him heated her up.

She had to forget about Chase Clements. *No telling what goes on down there at the river,* Alec had said. He was probably right. But she would never know, because she didn't care what was going on down there. At least, she kept telling herself that.

Maybe she had agreed to go out with Alec because he seemed safe and trustworthy. Or maybe it was because he was the type of man she *should* consider—if she were considering. Which she wasn't!

At any rate, a night out would be good for her. And, maybe, so would Alec.

But she didn't really believe that. She turned away from the door, thinking of Chase Clements, and how sexy he looked when he was soaking wet, sitting close to her in the deer blind.

3

SUNDAY AFTERNOON Suzanna dressed carefully. And casually. As much as she tried not to think of him, she couldn't keep Chase Clements out of her mind.

Tucking in her stomach, she zipped up her stone-washed jeans, tight. She slipped her feet into brown suede ankle boots, then pulled a pale blue bulky-knit sweater over her head. Surveying herself in the full-length mirror propped against the wall, she concluded that it was a look he'd probably like: casual.

The trip from their little cottage on the hill behind the Rutherford homeplace-turned-country-club to the Boon Docks took less than ten minutes to drive. That made Chase Clements very close.

Suzanna remembered the cluster of shacks that, ten years ago, had characterized the Clements place. The shacks had been replaced by log cabins set in a row along the river and used for rental. A larger building served as the center for renting and selling fishing equipment. Motorboats were moored to the pier that jutted into the White River. As she got out of her car, Suzanna glanced around, looking for Chase. He was nowhere in sight, and she breathed easier.

Before she and Ross reached the front steps, they were greeted by one of the biggest men she'd ever seen.

"Howdy, ma'am. You must be Suzanna." He shook her hand and turned to her son. "And I'll bet you're Ross." He shook Ross's hand, also.

The boy responded with a proud grin.

"You must have been expecting us," Suzanna said.

"Well, in a way. We weren't sure when you'd come." The big man shoved his cap back on his head and examined her with blatant curiosity.

"Ken said he invited Ross over today. Something about worms and fishing. You know kids. Chase said you'd probably tag along, too." He chuckled. "And he was right."

She stiffened. "Oh, he did, did he?"

"Yep. He said to watch out for you. Now I can see why."

"You seem to know a lot about us, but I don't think we've met."

"Excuse me, ma'am, but we have. It's been a few years and too many biscuits ago. I'm Bo Williams."

"Bo—" Suzanna started to laugh. "I can't believe it! You and I . . . we went to school together, remember?"

"Oh, yes. I couldn't forget you. Ever."

"Well, I must admit, Bo, I would never have recognized you." She smiled broadly. "You have certainly grown *up!*"

"You bet," he said with a sudden shy grin. "I outgrew the hogs 'n' the hosses."

"Do you remember the day we fought in third grade?"

"I always regretted that incident, but you were a spitfire. I hope I didn't hurt you too badly."

"You fought him, Mom?" Ross asked, intrigued by the conversation his mother was having with the hulking man.

"Can you believe it?" she said with a laugh. "We were both much smaller then. And I was much dumber! Please, Bo, call me Suzanna. No more of this 'ma'am' stuff."

Just then, someone called Ross's name, and they turned around to see a smaller version of Chase Clements approaching. "Ross! Glad you made it!"

Bo introduced Suzanna to Ken. He was a delightful kid with a quick smile and a confident attitude. She could see why Ross, who tended to be shy, had responded to him right away.

"Let's go meet my dad. Then we'll get some *primo* worms and go fishing! I'll show you the best trout holes." He led them to the side of the main building where Chase was working on a motorcycle.

Suzanna's breath caught in her throat at the sight of the lean, long-legged man in tight Levi's and a torn T-shirt. His hair straggled across his forehead, his chin wore the same reddish stubble as it had when they last met, and his face was intense with concentration. His muscular arms were streaked with grease and his hands were covered with the shiny black goo. Despite all that, he was damn attractive to her.

"Dad, they're here!"

Right away Suzanna knew that they had expected her and Ross. It irked her to think that Chase Clements, who barely knew her, could so easily predict what she was going to do.

Chase turned around and faced them. The tear in his shirt extended from the side seam diagonally across his chest, revealing a muscular stomach and a smattering of sandy-colored chest curls. He gave her a sweeping glance and a flicker of his eyes, then focused on Ross. "Hey! I'm Chase. Nice to make your acquaintance. I would shake hands, but I feel like 'Tar Baby.'"

Ross laughed, responding instantly to Chase's warmth.

"How do you like your new home?"

Ross shrugged. "It's okay."

"It'll probably take a while to get used to it. But Grace isn't such a bad place to be. Especially if you like the outdoors. Do you like to fish?"

"Don't know."

"You've never fished?" He shot Suzanna a quick, hard glare, as if it were her fault.

She opened her mouth to explain, but before she could speak, Chase continued. "Well, we'll fix that. Bo and Ken are experts on extracting trout from the White River. How'd you like to take home a nice two-pounder?"

"Great! Today?" Excitement edged Ross's voice.

"Sure! Why not?"

Ross glanced at Suzanna. "Okay, Mom?"

"I'll watch out for them, ma'am—uh, Suzanna," Bo said.

"Okay. For a little while." She smiled gently at the boys, who ran off before she could change her mind. Bo lumbered after them.

Suzanna's gaze trailed the boys, then returned to Chase. He was grinning at her. What was he thinking? Again she felt that powerful electricity drawing them together.

"Good kid," he said.

She nodded. "So's yours."

"For all he's been through, Ken's pretty secure."

"Ross is usually shy with strangers. But he and Ken seem to hit it off." She smiled slightly. "That's the happiest Ross has been all week."

"Bo'll make sure they're safe, if you're worried about the water, Suzanna." He grabbed a rag and began wiping the grease off his hands. "Does Ross know how to swim?"

"Yes."

"Good. They'll be fine. And have fun, I guarantee. That's what this place is all about."

"I was surprised to see Bo again. He's huge! I had no idea he worked for you."

"He's my general manager, jack-of-all-trades, and assists me in everything from watching after Ken to repairing the boat motors."

"He sounds like a great employee."

"He's more than an employee. Bo is like family." Chase pressed his lips together. "He's had his tough times, like the rest of us. But he's a good man. Loyal. Doesn't drink anymore. Helps me keep this place running." He dropped the dirty rag. "Come on in my office and let me get cleaned up. Then I'll show you around."

She walked behind him, trying not to pay attention to the way his jeans fit low on his hips . . . the way he swaggered with a masculine shifting of his body.

"I'm glad you came over here today, Suzanna," Chase said, stepping into a small office crammed full by a cluttered desk and an assortment of boxes. Pine-paneled walls were decorated with photos of fishermen proudly holding up their catch of the day.

She looked around. "It was Ross's idea to come."

Chase peeled off the torn T-shirt and began scrubbing his hands and arms up to the elbows with soap in the sink. "Oh, come on. You weren't just a little curious about this place? About me?"

"Not at all," she lied smoothly, trying to keep her eyes off his bare, hard-muscled torso. "I've been very busy this week. Far too busy to think of—"

"Of me?" He rinsed the soap and grease from his arms and picked up a towel.

"I've been getting settled at work. And we moved yesterday."

"You're looking good, Suzanna." He walked slowly toward her, drying his forearms and hands. "Real good. I expected you to drive over sooner than this."

"I hope you didn't place any bets on it."

"Naw. It was more fun to just see how long it would take you. And it didn't take long." He halted near her, and his clean smell drifted over them.

Suzanna swallowed hard and tried to keep her composure. She tried to pretend that he wore a shirt and that the sight of his bare chest wasn't so alluring.

"Do you expect me to believe that you didn't think of me once all week? Not even one night when you were over there all alone?" He paused, and his brown eyes took in her blue sweater, the slender hips beneath her jeans, the long legs that seemed to go on forever. His gaze swept back up to her eyes.

"Believe it." She wouldn't give him the satisfaction of knowing that she'd given him a second's thought. Nor that this scrutiny bothered her for one moment.

He smiled. Her dark, sleek hair was so intriguing the way it parted on one side and dipped toward the other eyebrow. He felt an urge to run his fingers through it. "Well, I thought about you all week," he admitted. "Every night."

"You must be bored then."

"I'm not as busy as you, that's for sure. But the things I do are for Ken and me. This is the life-style I've chosen."

"I thought it was the only life you knew."

"I've been around enough to experience others. And like you, when the times got tough, I headed back for Grace."

For some reason, she grew defensive. "I did it for Ross."

"Sure. And your mother."

"Yes. So, what's wrong with that?"

"It isn't truthful. Why don't you just admit it? You came back because *you* wanted to." He turned quickly and strode across the room.

"Okay." She folded her arms and watched him don a clean shirt that he'd pulled out of the bottom desk drawer. "I came back because this is where I felt most secure. When my life became frazzled, this is where I ran. Satisfied?"

"I like honesty, Suzanna. That's why this town and I don't get along very well."

"Are you saying you're the only one who's honest in Grace?"

"No. Now there's you. I'm still trying to understand, though, why you'd stoop to work for a jerk like Rutherford."

Suzanna felt her cheeks flare with anger. "I needed a good-paying job."

"And the one you took with Rutherford is?"

"With the added benefit of living on the grounds, yes."

The afternoon sun outlined his lean body with a golden glow. The black shirt he'd pulled on framed his broad shoulders and hugged his trim waist. He nodded slowly. "You're claiming there's truth to the old saying, 'Grace is a good place to live, but a tough place to make a living'?"

"It's especially true for women." She eyed him steadily. She wasn't about to back down from her convictions. It had been too hard to get this far. "I'm lucky to have my job. And proud of it."

Amused by her strong defense, he raised his eyebrow. "And I'm lucky you're living so close. Even though I think your judgment on choosing a boss is impaired."

"I didn't choose a boss. I accepted a job. We all have to eat, don't we? And I'm responsible for my son. Just because you don't happen to get along with Old Man Rutherford means nothing to me."

"I guess that clears the air, then." Chase hooked his thumbs into his front pockets. "How about that tour of the Boon Docks now?"

"Fine." She expected a quick walk around the modest buildings, not a ride on the wild side.

The next thing she knew he was saying "Let's try out the Harley. We can tour and have fun at the same time."

Worse yet, she was responding "Okay." Later she wondered why in heaven's name she'd agreed to ride with him. It seemed like fun. And a little wild. And she couldn't resist the two. Or maybe she just couldn't resist Chase Clements.

He straddled the big machine and revved it to life with one slash of his heel. He handed her a helmet, and she crawled behind him as if she'd done this all her life. Her hips slid close to his, her thighs aligned with his, her belly pressed to the small of his back.

"Hook your arms around me," he instructed above the roar of the engine.

She complied, attaching her hands to the taut muscles of his stomach, pressing her breasts to his back. He felt hard-bodied, secure, invincible, and she clung to him for dear life. It was frightening. And exciting. And she knew those were just a few of the reasons she'd said she'd go along with him.

They passed the pier and waved to Bo and the boys standing at the far end. They rolled alongside the row of log cabins for rent and past the larger one at the end, which Chase pointed to as his home. "Move *with* me," he instructed above the engine's roar. "When I lean, you lean."

"Right." She clung to his back, trying to sense his movements and do the same.

Then he shifted gears and the vehicle lurched forward to zoom down the dirt road in a cloud of dust. Exhilaration surged through Suzanna, and she felt like shouting.

The wind buffeted her face until a few strands of her hair wriggled loose from the helmet. Cool air worked through the loose knit of her sweater, and she huddled closer behind him.

Through blurry eyes, she watched the silver-gray river and orange-red trees whiz past. He leaned into a turn, and she angled her body with his. "Move with me," he'd said. And she did.

They rode away from the river, entering an ever-green forest. The rich, clean smell of pine surrounded them. A dark green canopy covered them, and a heavy cushion of brown needles softened their path, muffling the sound of the engine. Chase had whisked her away, and they were alone, completely alone. Suzanna clung even more tightly to him.

Finally their chariot slowed and rolled to a stop. Chase snapped off the noisy engine, and there was silence. They sat quiet and motionless for a few minutes. The vibrations from the engine continued to throb through their bodies. It was a wildly sensuous experience.

He shifted both his legs to the ground. His thighs moved against hers. "Suzanna?"

She raised her head from his back and looked around. "Where are we?"

"Downstream. A little cove. It's pretty. Want to walk around?"

With effort, she swung her leg over the machine and stood alone. Suddenly she felt cold and shaky without his support, without his body next to hers. She took a few steps, trying to disconnect herself from this man who had managed to revive her youthful fantasies of them together.

He walked quietly beside her.

"This is beautiful, Chase." She took a deep breath. "Where are we?"

"Near the back nine." He waved his arm in an arc. "Over there's Rutherford's. This is part of the property that he claimed was his.

She pointed to a few bare-branched trees that grew in rows in a low field near the river. "Those look like pecan trees."

"Yep. The last stragglers of an old pecan grove. The main part was on Rutherford's property, and he had them all leveled for the golf course a few years ago." His voice lowered to a bitter monotone. "That's progress."

"That's capitalism. He probably figured the country club with its golf course was more valuable than an old past-its-prime pecan orchard."

"Yeah." Chase chuckled. "A few natural nuts in trees exchanged for a bunch of golfing nuts walking these fields in colored pants."

"What would you rather have?" she countered. "A bunch of guys wading the river in hip boots and losing their expensive lures in tree branches?"

"I'd rather have the nuts. The real ones."

She looked at him pointedly. "I heard you threatened Mr. Rutherford."

"I did."

She stopped and drew in her breath. Chase seemed so nonviolent and forthright to her. Those elements were part of the undeniable attraction she felt for him. And now he was admitting to the rumors that she'd discounted?

"Old Man Rutherford promised to sue me and challenge my claim to the land. He said some rough things about my father, most of which were probably true, but it angered me to hear him say them. He said that my dad never owned this land outright. I told him that was a lie and if he took me to court, he'd live to regret it."

"Did you threaten to hurt him?"

"Of course not! I meant that he'd be proven wrong. My intention is to sue, if it comes to that. The land's mine, fair and square, and I shouldn't have to defend it."

"Well, I guess that constitutes a threat of sorts."

"I simply called his bluff. Notice he never filed suit?"

They grew quiet again and walked around the cove, side by side. Occasionally their arms touched, sparking a tremendous surge of desire between them. But they didn't show it. They just kept walking.

At the water's edge, Chase found a spot to sit under an old oak. The bare branches spread in all directions with several stretching over the water. A few crimson leaves remained and occasionally one would fall, drifting slowly to earth or land on the water and float away. Chase picked up an acorn top and whirled it into the water. "I come here sometimes to relax. Sometimes to think."

"It's very peaceful. I can see why it's a good spot for that."

He motioned over his shoulder to Rutherford's land. "Then you can see why I find the little men in colored pants roaming those fields disturbing."

Suzanna joined Chase under the tree, sitting cross-legged. "Yes. You want your peace and quiet."

"Rutherford can do whatever he wants with his land and there's not a damn thing I can do about it, even though I find it offensive."

"But so can you."

He looked at her with a prideful little grin. "You're right. This is my land. It's one of the few good things my old man left for his kids. And I intend to see that we all enjoy it."

"What about Darlene? Is she banned?"

"Absolutely not! If she came back tomorrow, she could move right in."

"What would you do about Ken?"

Chase brooded for a moment and tossed a couple of acorns into the water. "I'd do whatever was best for Ken. She's his mother. He knows that. He also knows who's taken care of him."

"And who loves him," Suzanna added softly. "That's very evident, Chase."

"He's a real good kid. Nothing like I was when I was his age."

"You *were* quite a devil," she admitted with a little chuckle. "Maybe not at eleven."

"Ah, I was well on my way by then. I had a lot to rebel against, and started early." He lifted his chin and gazed steadily at her. There were no apologies in his expression. He'd made a statement, and as far as he was concerned, that justified his actions.

She supposed he might be right. Looking over at him, she wondered if this was the same Chase Clements who once placed a live frog in old Miss Renner's desk drawer and howled with laughter when it jumped out in her face and made her cry.

Suzanna liked the hard-angled planes of his face. They revealed Chase as a person experienced in life, a survivor of both good and tough times. But the unruly way his hair curled over his forehead and the way his brown eyes twinkled indicated that he knew how to have fun, to enjoy the moment. She found those elements about him enticing.

"You've changed a lot, Chase."

"You really think so?"

"Maybe I just never knew you before."

"I was never one to follow the crowd. That's the fellow you knew. The rebel."

"Yes, a maverick. But I understand. We both have rebellious natures. I just ran away from mine, while you've manufactured a very nice life around yours."

"I don't know that I've analyzed it quite like that before. I'm simply me. Being a river rat, I was never cut out to wear suits and ties every day and be trapped inside a building. I've always rejected the easy way. Always had to do it my way—which, more often than not, turned out to be the hard way."

Suzanna understood the need. It was probably behind her decision to run away with Zack eleven years ago. "I have a confession to make, Chase."

He settled back against the base of the tree and grinned at her. "Already? And we've only just met again."

"It has to do with my bringing Ross over here."

"You didn't want him to come, did you?"

"No, I didn't." Her blue-gray eyes met his gaze with straight honesty. "And my reasoning was based on rumor. Not facts. I was judging your son on your past behavior. And you on your father's. That isn't fair."

"What made you change your mind and come anyway?"

"Out of the mouths of babes." She shrugged. "Ross made me see what I was doing. He said I didn't even know Ken. And he was right."

"I'm downright disappointed."

"What?"

"I wanted you to say you couldn't wait to see me again."

She smiled and looked away. "Do you think I'd admit it, even if it were so? Which it isn't!"

"No, I suppose you wouldn't, Suzanna." He reached down and picked up her hand, which rested on the ground near his leg. Her skin felt soft, and he caressed the top with his thumb. "That would be expecting too much. And I never expect too much."

Suzanna longed to take him in her arms but she held back.

"That sweater matches your eyes," he said softly.

"And your eyes are like . . ." *Did she dare say "like a tiger when he's ready to pounce"?* ". . . are honest. Can I believe them, Chase?"

"Believe everything they tell you." His eyes danced teasingly as he dropped her hand to his thigh and placed his large hand over hers. "A bluegrass group from Little Rock is performing in Grace next week. Would you like to attend? You can bring Ross. There'll be a barbecue before and dancing afterward."

"Sounds great!" She felt dry-mouthed and fiery. "When is it?"

"Saturday night."

"Oh." There was a definite downcast tone to her voice. "I'm sorry, but I can't."

"Don't you like bluegrass music?"

"Yes, but I already have plans."

He gazed at her with a sardonic smile. "A date?"

"I'm busy, that's all." She pulled her hand away from its sensual contact with his leg.

"Ahh, it *is* a date."

She could feel the heat building as those sparks started between them again. "So what? I'm not a hermit, you know."

He aimed a thumb at his chest. "I couldn't care less what you do with your time. Or who you spend it with."

"Then why are we discussing it?"

He shrugged and shook his head. "Beats me. Do you have a reliable sitter for Ross?"

She tossed her head. "Mama volunteered. Is she reliable enough?"

"Yeah. Sure."

"They're going out for pizza." Suzanna pretended to remain casual. "She's trying to get to know him, to relate to her nine-year-old grandson who she barely knows. They have a lot of catching up to do."

"I feel the same way about us." Chase smiled at her. It was a taunting smile as his gaze traveled over her face. Something in his arrogant expression infuriated her and, at the same time, inflamed her. She wished he'd touch her face in that same sensual way with his hands . . . or with his lips.

"Why?"

"I don't know. Somehow I feel that we never had a fair chance."

"And now we do?"

"We would, if you'd give it a chance."

"I'm here, aren't I?"

"And I keep wondering why," he said. He reached up and traced her cheek with his forefinger. Her skin was like silk.

"Me, too."

"I didn't notice any resistance on your part."

She sighed. "But I shouldn't—"

"Let me guess. Is it Alec McNeil?"

She sat upright. "You don't let up, do you?"

"I just wonder who's beating my time, that's all."

"Your time?"

"Someday, Suzanna, your time will be my time."

"You're crazy!"

"Crazy like a fox. I'm betting on it!" He laughed.

"We'd better go. It's getting late." She strode back to where the motorcycle was parked and waited until he ambled over. His dark eyes met hers and momentarily locked with them—making daring, seductive promises.

She looked away.

He stood before her. With one finger he lifted her chin. "Suz-anna . . ."

She raised her eyes in time to see his face descending toward hers. She felt the faintest whisper of a kiss, his lips brushing hers with soft strokes. Then he clamped his lips on hers, hard and passionately. The stubble of a beard around his mouth scraped her tender skin and set off an ache of longing through her.

As quickly as it had happened, the kiss was over, and he was sitting astride the cycle, handing her a helmet. With shaky hands, she adjusted it, then clasped her arms around his waist.

"Move with me . . ."

They drove into the wind. Dazed, Suzanna could still hear his laughter. The sound echoed in her mind as they rode fast to beat the wind. She pressed her face to his back and again felt the softness of his lips on hers before the onslaught of his kiss.

All of a sudden Chase yelled, and the bike swerved. The cycle bumped and zigzagged across the road, then shook and whirled around madly. Suzanna clung tightly to Chase. She could hear him saying *Go with me . . . go with me,* as they flew through the air.

4

THEY LANDED HARD.

Tumbling ungracefully, in a tangle of arms and legs, they came to a stop still hooked together. Suzanna lay prone over Chase, her left arm clutching his waist. The arm stung.

She lifted her head. Feeling weak and dizzy, she dropped her forehead back to his chest. He was strong, solid, and—oh, Lord—not moving.

Her body felt shaken and achy. Her chest was tight, and it was a struggle to draw a breath. Slowly the breathing got better. So did the dizziness. Gingerly, she began to move each limb. No sharp pains. Nothing broken. Just dull aches everywhere. At least she was alive and moving.

But what about Chase? He lay perfectly still on his back. Under her.

Heart pounding, Suzanna stared at him, looking closely for signs of breathing. What if—oh, my God!— he were dead! And she was here. There'd be no denying that she'd been riding on that motorcycle in the woods with Chase Clements.

What was wrong with her, caring what others thought? Caring who knew she was with him? She had denied to him that she gave a tinker's damn about his reputation. Hers wasn't pristine, either. Now all she cared about was if he were alive. She pressed her ear to his chest. His heartbeat was slow and steady. *Thank you, God! He's alive!*

She pulled her arm from under him and examined the painful area. The lower sleeve of her blue sweater was ripped to shreds and her forearm was covered with bloody scratches. She decided that she'd come out of the wreck lucky if this was her only injury.

Suzanna turned her attention back to Chase. She removed her helmet to get a better look at him. Watching him closely, she thought she detected slight movement.

He groaned.

Thank God, he's breathing!

Suzanna wasn't sure if her exultation came from sheer happiness that he was alive or relief that they wouldn't be caught together. Her hypocrisy was disgraceful. She hated it, and yet she felt obligated to follow the standard of the town. At least she was trying.

Emitting another low groan, Chase reached up and pushed the helmet off his head. He lay there, eyes closed, lips slightly open, growllike sounds vibrating from his throat. His strong profile—the aquiline nose, the lower lip that curved to match the upper, and square chin covered with stubble—stood out in contrast to the rough, dusty surface of the road. From the pale, translucent skin of his eyelids sprouted the most thick and luscious eyelashes she'd seen on a man. She knew—and recalled the feeling with pleasure—the way those soft lips felt on hers: *sensual and warm.*

She hovered anxiously over his still form, touching his face. What would she do if he were hurt badly? "Chase?" She raised her voice. "Chase, can you hear me?"

Another, louder groan came from deep in his chest.

Excitedly Suzanna grabbed his shoulders and squeezed hard. "Oh, please, Chase! Wake up! Speak to me!"

"Mmmfff . . ." He was beginning to mumble incoherently, but his eyes remained closed.

"Chase . . ." She framed his cheeks with both her hands. His skin felt cool, and he looked dark against her pale fingers. Beneath her frantic caress, he was pliant but prickly where he hadn't shaved—a real man, not some leathery roughneck. Touching him was pleasurable.

Finally his eyelids flickered, and she held her breath. She moved closer, staring down at him, *willing* him to open up, to become alert, to be himself again.

The late-afternoon sun was starting to slip behind the bank of green pines. She had to get him out of here. And she had to get home. "Chase, wake up! Oh, please . . ."

His eyelids opened halfway, then all the way. He blinked at her a couple of times. Dark eyes focused on the slender, raven-haired woman who lay across his body, her intense gray eyes anxiously staring, her face inches from his.

"Can you see me, Chase?"

No, get closer. He took a deep breath. His arms closed automatically around her back. "I must have died and gone to heaven."

"Are you . . . all right?" She knew it was a dumb question, but she wanted him to talk, needed to elicit a response from him.

"Don't know."

"How do you feel?"

"Pretty good." His answer was better than she'd expected.

"Oh, thank goodness," she breathed, then demanded, "See if you can move everything!" Were those beautiful eyes of his focusing?

"I'd rather lie right here, just like this."

"See if anything's broken."

Slowly he obliged, pressing her with one arm, then the other. One leg moved, then the other, shifting her to nestle in the vee of his spread-apart legs. "Most everything seems to be in working order," he mumbled.

She felt another movement, an almost imperceptible rocking of his hips. "Oh—" She tried to get up.

"Don't move." His arms tightened around her. "I may need your help."

"Oh ... You devil! And I was really worried about you!"

"I'm worried, too. We have to see if everything is working."

"You need your head examined!"

"*That* isn't what I need examined."

She pushed against his chest, finally extricating herself from his grasp. "Well, you can check out *all* your body parts with someone else! Not me!" She struggled to her feet and staggered unsteadily backward.

"You okay, Suz?" He propped himself up on one elbow and looked at her.

"A lot you care!"

"I do. I—" He sat up in the dust, trying to convince her with his serious expression.

When he stood, she saw that his T-shirt was ripped. Suddenly she was concerned about him again. "Oh,

Chase, turn around. Your shirt is torn. What about your back?" Dutifully he turned around for her inspection. She lifted the shredded shirt and examined his muscular shoulders and back. "One long scrape," she assessed, trying to remain matter-of-fact, "and several small cuts."

He wriggled his shoulders and arched his back. "God, I'm sore already."

"Probably bruised, too." She watched the muscles flex and ripple beneath his roughed-up skin.

"No big deal. At least, we're both all right."

"We . . . we need to get back. Ross'll be concerned about me."

"Yeah." He stooped to pick up his helmet. Then, with a casualness that she admired, Chase draped his arm around her shoulders and steered her toward the downed motorcycle. He straddled the vehicle and looked at her. "Ready?"

She nodded and let out a deep sigh. They were lucky not to have been seriously hurt, and that realization was settling in on her, leaving her shaky.

He reached for her hand, only then noticing the scratches on her arm. "My God, Suz! What happened to you?"

"It's just a few scrapes and bruises."

He examined her arm with a furrowed brow that seemed very out of place on Chase's face. When he looked up at her, his eyes were serious. "We'll fix you up at my house." Then he motioned for her to sit in the groove behind him.

They were going to his place. Hesitating only a moment, Suzanna threw her leg over the machine and nestled against the natural curve of his lean body. He spurred the motor to life and, in another few minutes, they were off—slowly this time, but moving ahead.

When they arrived at Chase's quaint cabin, they helped each other inside. Her arm circled his waist, and his arm draped over her shoulder as they climbed the few steps to the porch. He showed her where the key was hidden and unlocked the door.

"Now you know the secret hiding place of my key and can enter my home at will." He chuckled. "I just hope you will after this."

"Not under these circumstances again, I hope." She scanned the sparse room. It lacked any sign of a feminine hand, but still had a certain warmth. And as the home of a bachelor father and a young boy, it certainly was comfortable and acceptably neat.

With their arms still around each other, they stood in the middle of the room for a prolonged moment, each reluctant to let go, each reluctant to admit it. He gazed apologetically at her arm. "Suzanna, I'm sorry about this."

"It was an accident. Don't worry about me. You're scratched up, too."

"I'll be okay. Just got a helluva headache. And my back feels raw."

"It's that long scratch. We need to clean it."

"And your arm." He hobbled stiffly across the room. "Let's see. Come in the kitchen where the light is better."

They scrutinized each other's injuries. "First we have to get rid of this dirt," Suzanna observed.

"A shower," he agreed, then added hopefully, "Together?"

She gave him an incredulous look. "Are you okay, Chase?"

"Why don't you come in with me, just to make sure I don't get dizzy or something?"

Folding her arms across her breasts, she drawled, "And what would I be able to do if you suddenly got dizzy?"

"Help me to bed," he quickly explained.

She shook her head and fought back a smile. "If you can't shower alone, forget it for now. I'll just use a clean cloth on your back."

"Spoilsport," he grumbled as he made his way to the bathroom.

While he showered, she rinsed her arm under the faucet, then fixed them a pot of coffee.

He returned shortly, wearing clean Levi's with no shirt and no socks. Suzanna struggled for composure. She dabbed his back with the antiseptic he provided. When she had finished, she poured their cups of coffee.

"Now, your turn. Let me see your arm." With large but gentle hands he sprinkled her forearm with the antiseptic. "This is terrible, Suzanna. It's been years since I took a spill like that. And never with a lady."

"Do you know what actually happened?"

He rubbed his face with one hand. "A family of raccoons crossed my path. Can you believe that? They just popped out of the weeds. We must have scared them, because usually they avoid people."

"I never saw them. Things were happening too fast." Actually, her face had been buried against his shoulder as she fantasized about him.

"I knew that if I hit those animals, I'd lose control for sure. But when I tried to dodge them, the thick dust on the road threw me into a spin." He took her hand and caressed it. "I feel terrible about this, Suzanna."

"You took the brunt of the fall, Chase. Your back is worse than my arm. How do you feel now?"

"Better. I'm okay."

"Well, then, I need to be going."

"I'll call Bo to come and get you." He walked over to the phone and punched seven numbers. After a brief exchange, he returned to her, standing so close that he could smell her alluring fragrance mingled with their body heat. He wanted her more than ever, and yet he knew it couldn't be now. Bracing one arm on the wall above her shoulder, he touched her arm. "Suzanna, I'm really sorry about the accident."

"I know. You've already said that, Chase."

"I don't often apologize to women."

"I'll bet."

"It's too bad about your sweater." He touched the knit. "Ruined."

She felt his fingers caressing the material. "Want to know something funny? I wore it—" she paused self-consciously "—for you, Chase."

"For me?"

"After what you said about my eyes, I wore blue because I know it makes my eyes darker."

"You wanted to get my attention?"

"I guess." Her voice was barely a whisper.

"Suzanna, you got my attention from that first day I found you wading in the river. I've done nothing but think of those gorgeous eyes of yours since then." He moved closer and, almost tentatively, lowered his face until he kissed her lips.

"For a man who claimed to be so dizzy that you needed help standing in the shower, you found your mark quite well."

"Instinct. When I'm close to you, my senses are on red alert."

She chuckled a little nervously at his continued closeness. "Another first, Chase. I've never heard that line, either."

"And I've never felt quite like this." He lifted her hand to his lips and pressed a quick kiss on the palm before dropping it with a loud sigh. "I hear Bo's truck." He moved so she could leave.

She walked briskly across the room, then stopped at the door. "Thanks for the tour. It's been an...interesting afternoon, Chase." She meant intriguing, alluring, exciting, wild, sexy—everything except "interesting." And yet, *interesting* was the only word that she could say.

"Even if it did end in disaster?"

"We're okay, and that's what counts."

He nodded and lifted one hand, more in a gesture than a wave. "Come back any time. Bring Ross." The image of the dark-haired beauty with the torn sleeve was imprinted clearly on his mind.

"I'll be seeing you, Chase." Suzanna quickly turned and walked to the waiting truck. She crawled into the seat that Ken vacated, wondering if she actually would see Chase again. She had no plans to. And if she knew what was good for her, she would stay away. He was nothing but trouble.

"Hey, Mom! What happened to you?" Ross exclaimed when he saw her arm.

"Oh, it's just a scratch." Her gaze went over Ross's head and met Bo's. "We, uh, had a spill on the cycle."

Bo's gaze hardened, and she answered his unasked question. "Chase's back is scratched pretty bad. But he's okay, I think." A man who managed to kiss the way he had in the cottage had to be all right.

Ross could contain his excitement no longer. "Wait'll you see the fish I caught! Bo's going to cook it for us!"

She smiled wanly at Bo. The thought of smelling fish right now brought on a wave of nausea.

SUZANNA TRIED to dismiss the erotic thoughts of Chase that had plagued her all night. But he'd been on her mind all day at work, too, as she wondered how he was feeling and if he'd been to a doctor. She was even thinking of him the next afternoon when she drove to her mother's house to pick up Ross. Once again, she found herself caught in the middle of a family argument.

"You don't understand, Gramma Ellie! This is a chance to have some *fun!*"

"Oh, I understand, Ross. You're saying that coming over here after school isn't fun." Ellie sat with her hands clutched together in her lap.

"It's fun here. But this will be *more fun!*" Enthusiasm made his voice squeak.

"So, go ahead and do it." Ellie's tone was low and full of pain. "I can manage just fine. Alone."

"Do *what*, Mama?" Suzanna looked from her mother to her son. "Ross?"

"Look, Mom. All you have to do is sign this paper. Here." He thrust two mimeographed pages into her hands. "This will explain all about after-school sports!"

Suzanna read the papers.

"Everybody's doing it! Even Ken. Right now they're playing football. Then it'll be basketball. Then volleyball and in the spring, soccer. Sounds great, huh?"

"Yes, it does." Suzanna looked down at her son. His face was lit with excitement. Clearly this was something he really wanted to do. And something he probably needed to do to help him adjust in the new school. She looked over at her mother.

The light so recently glowing in Ellie's eyes was gone. She was hurt by the new turn of events, but reticent. Suzanna tried to make the situation less hurtful for her mother. "Maybe we need to evaluate this, Ross."

"I knew it!" he said angrily. "You'll find something wrong with playing sports with my new friends. Next thing I know, we'll be moving!"

"No, we aren't moving." Suzanna took him by the shoulders. "Ross, why don't you go watch TV while I talk with Mama a few minutes? Then we'll discuss this at home."

"She'll talk you out of it," he told her sullenly.

"No, I won't, Ross, sugar. All I want is for you to be happy." Ellie sighed loudly and walked toward the kitchen.

Suzanna groaned mentally. Her mother's tone dripped with self-pity, designed to make everyone else feel guilty. She gave Ross a silent command with her eyes and pointed toward the TV. "Please. We'll go home soon." Even at this moment, she'd prefer for him to be out playing sports with the kids than inside watching

TV. She followed her mother into the old-fashioned kitchen.

Ellie fiddled with the stove. "Lemon tea?"

"Yes, please." Suzanna took a seat at the old walnut pedestal table. This was where she and her brother, Butch, had spent many hours for everything from family meals to games with friends to homework. It was also where she'd told her mother she was leaving with Zack eleven years ago. Now she was back here with her son, and it was a good feeling. Acting as a go-between, however, was not a part of her happy image of life "back home."

While waiting for her mother to serve the tea, she re-read the papers that explained the after-school sports program.

"I know the man who's leading this." Ellie set two porcelain cups on the table. "Ray Montgomery is doing a good job, I'm sure."

Suzanna laid the papers aside. "Then why are you objecting, Mama?"

"I'm not. I want what's best for my grandson." When she sat down, she looked thoroughly dejected. "Ross just let me know that I'm not needed anymore. And I can't help my feelings."

"Of course you can't, Mama—if that were true, which it isn't. You *are* needed in our lives. Maybe not for keeping him after school, though."

"Obviously not."

"But, Mama, you know how kids are. They're always off doing their own thing. I don't want you to think you aren't wanted and needed. You are. That's why we came back. We all need our families." She patted her mother's blue-veined hand, but in spite of her strong verbal assurances and physical demonstrations of love, Suzanna left her mother's house, feeling guilty about the turn of events.

She and Ross hadn't been home ten minutes that night when Bo Williams called and asked to speak to Ross. Suzanna tried not to pay attention to Ross's side of the conversation, but she couldn't miss his enthusiasm.

He hung up and bounced into her bedroom. "Mom! Bo invited me over for a fish supper with Ken tonight. We're going to cook the fish we caught yesterday! Can I go?"

"Now? Tonight?"

"Yeah." Ross's face was animated. "We caught them. It's only fair that we get to eat them! Okay?"

"Well . . ." Her thoughts went immediately to Chase and she wondered how he was feeling. Here was her chance to find out.

"Come on, say okay! Ken's already over there."

She studied Ross for a few seconds. He was so happy, he could hardly stand still. "Okay, you can go for a little while. But just long enough to eat, do you understand? This is a school night, and I'm sure you have homework."

"All right! I'll call him back and tell him!" He bounded out of the room.

"Ross, how are you getting there?"

"Bo said he'd come in a little while and get me if you couldn't take me over."

She thought a minute. "I'll take you."

"Okay!" Ross dashed from the room and accepted Bo's invitation. He chatted all the way over to the Boon

Docks about eating the very fish he caught and how he wanted to go fishing again next weekend.

Suzanna dropped Ross off at the back portion of the main building where Bo lived. "I'll be back in an hour. Be ready. And no arguments."

"Yes, Mom." He skipped to the door, the argument with his grandmother forgotten. Bo opened the door, and Ken appeared by his side. They waved to Suzanna, then disappeared inside.

The trouble with adults, Suzanna decided, was that they couldn't forget the problems and personalities of everyone in their realm. But kids could joyfully go on to the next activity without looking back. Suzanna couldn't forget her mother's dejected expression when they'd left her tonight. Nor could she forget Chase and the way he'd made her feel when his lips met hers.

She had limited Ross to an hour's suppertime and, by doing so, had imposed the same time limit on herself. But that would be more than enough to see how Chase was feeling. And that's all she wanted to do.

He opened the door at her first knock. He wore a button-down-collar shirt hanging loosely over his jeans. To Suzanna, he looked marvelously sexy. Perhaps she shouldn't even go inside the house with him.

Smiling wickedly at her, he stepped back. "I see you couldn't stay away."

She hesitated. "I merely came to see how you're feeling."

"Like hell. Sore all over. And you?"

Chase certainly wasn't one to hide anything. Maybe that's why she loved talking to him. He was refreshingly blunt. She stepped inside the warm room. "Not too bad."

He stood facing her, his broad-shouldered form backlit by a fire. "I feel like someone beat me up and threw me back. I ache from the inside out. Otherwise, I'm fine." His gaze settled softly on her, and he smiled slightly.

She grinned sheepishly. "I've had some of the same problems today. I just couldn't tell anybody about them. It's nice to be able to complain to someone who understands."

"You didn't want anyone knowing you were over here yesterday, did you?"

She hedged. "Well, the only people I saw were Mr. Rutherford and my mother. I figured it was neither one's business." She paused. "I brought Ross to Bo's for a fish dinner tonight."

"I heard about the great fish fry. Have you eaten?"

She shook her head. "I just got home from work."

"You work this late?"

"I had to go pick up Ross at Mama's. And we had to get a little problem settled."

"She isn't ill, is she?"

"No, she's fine. She just had an argument with Ross. As usual, I got caught in the middle."

He motioned toward the kitchen. "Come tell me about it while we fix supper."

Before she knew it, Suzanna had taken off her jacket and was tearing lettuce for a salad and telling Chase about her latest frustrations. "I feel as though I set Mama up for this fall. She was so happy to be keeping Ross every day. And he was satisfied to stay with her."

"Until something better came along."

"Sounds cruel, doesn't it?" She chopped the celery with fast, hard strokes.

"No. It sounds normal for a kid." He put a hearty sandwich on each plate. "Look where our kids are tonight: off doing something that sounds like it's better than staying home eating turkey sandwiches with us."

"You're right." She took a seat at the table. "Ross enjoys being with Mama and hearing stories of the old days when we were kids. Actually, I think he's missed having family around all these years."

Chase gave them each a cup of coffee and joined her. "I'm sure he has."

"But she thinks he doesn't care for her now that he has this chance to play football." Suzanna sighed. "Trouble is, she doesn't have enough activity to fill her life. We're pretty much it."

"And you feel guilty." He took a bite and motioned for her to start. "You can't be responsible for her happiness, Suz."

"I know. I'm trying to get her interested in something besides us. That might help."

"Sounds like a good plan." They ate in silence for a few minutes. He startled her with his warmth and understanding. "I'm glad you decided to come over tonight, Suzanna. Surprised, though."

"Why?"

"After I nearly killed you."

"We . . . I guess we were lucky, Chase."

"Yep. Very."

"Actually, I had something else to discuss with you."

"What's that?"

Suzanna took another bite. "This sandwich is delicious. Special sauce?"

"Horseradish. I add it to practically everything. Works like a charm. The salad's great, too, Suzanna."

"Must be the way I tear lettuce." She laughed. "It's my specialty."

"You had something else on your mind?"

"Business. Would you consider selling wholesale fish to the country club?"

"Sure. We make a lot of commercial fish sales."

"Before we discuss anything specific, I'd like to have a pricing brochure for comparison."

"Sure. I'll send you one tomorrow."

"Terrific. It would be so convenient if you could provide some of our products. I'm interviewing potential chefs tomorrow, and I'll know after that what kind of foods he or she wants to fix, and how much we'll need."

They finished eating, and she helped him clean up while discussing the different types of fish he could provide and approximate costs per hundred pounds.

Finally she checked her watch. "I'd better go. Told Ross I'd pick him up soon."

Chase touched her hand. When she didn't pull away, he laced his fingers through hers, pulling her closer. "Tell me the truth, Suzanna. Why did you really come over here?"

"I had to bring Ross."

"Didn't *have* to. Bo would have come after him." He felt her arm rub against his, and he longed to touch more of her. "The truth, Suz."

"I . . . wanted to discuss the fish business." She felt drawn to him, and when she caught his subtle mossy scent, her mind wandered from business to their sexual chemistry.

"You could have done that over the phone."

"I . . . wanted to see how you were."

With slow deliberation, he drew her into his arms. Her willpower evaporated as soon as she felt his strong, lean body against hers.

"And how am I?" His lips moved dangerously close to hers.

"I meant, uh, how you were feeling after the wreck. Your head and your back." Suzanna felt herself melt into the strength and comfort of his arms.

"My head is a little crazy these days. I keep thinking about a certain dark-haired lady from my past, and what it would be like to make love to her."

"Chase!"

"It's the truth, Suzanna. I can't help it. As for my back, it's pretty messed up, but still strong enough for—"

"Please, don't say it." His lips brushed hers.

"Well, we couldn't have done this business over the phone."

"Chase . . ." Suddenly it no longer seemed necessary to fight the sensations that surged through her whenever they were together. Now they were alone, pressed together, and she didn't have to hold anything back. Maybe, just this once, she could enjoy.

When she relaxed in his embrace, his lips closed firmly over hers. Without hesitation his tongue sought the sweet inner recesses of her mouth, and she willingly opened to him. Never had a kiss penetrated her with such intensity.

Reluctantly, he lifted his lips from hers. "Oh, Suzanna, what you do to me."

She whispered his name: "Chase—" She wouldn't dare admit what his kiss did to her. Not even to herself.

"The truth, Suz. You came for this, didn't you?"

"Y-yes." Her voice was low. "I . . . I couldn't stay away."

He leaned back and looked at her. "You tried to?"

"Yes. Oh, my, yes! I'm still trying."

"I'm trying, too." With a low laugh, he kissed her again. His hands framed and lifted her breasts while his thumbs caressed the hard-nippled tips beneath her clothes. His mouth possessed hers, firmly, sensually.

Placing her palms on his chest, she forced them apart. "Chase, I . . . I have to go."

"Don't—"

"I can't stay. I was supposed to pick up Ross—" she checked her watch "—half an hour ago."

"I can call Bo and delay—"

"No. I can't. This is . . . too much already."

"You, Suzanna, are never enough for me. We have to have more, don't you see that?"

"No, Chase. I'd better go." She grabbed her purse and made her way to the door. She knew she should leave but didn't want to. It was totally crazy.

"Suzanna?"

She halted and looked at him, his disheveled hair across his forehead, his eyes dark with passion. "I'll send that price list tomorrow."

She nodded and smoothed her hair on one side. Then she was gone, not looking back, trying to tell herself this was *it*. No more times alone with Chase. This could have led to more, very easily, very quickly. She couldn't let it happen. *She just couldn't!* Chase wasn't the kind of man for her. He was trouble! Too independent. Too much of a rebel. She couldn't trust him.

But she couldn't trust herself, either. She knew, just as surely as the sun would rise tomorrow over the Arkansas pines, that she'd be back.

Suzanna glanced at the house and saw Chase's form outlined in the window. He stood in the darkened living room, watching her.

He knew, too, that she'd be back.

5

"YOU DID *WHAT*?"

Suzanna blinked as she gazed through Mr. Rutherford's cigar-smoke screen. "Alec McNeil seems to have the best deal on wholesale pork and beef."

"No, no. Repeat the part about Clements."

"I'm considering buying our fish wholesale from Chase Clements. He definitely has the best prices."

Rutherford's face flushed. "I should say not!"

"Actually, I understood that purchasing was to be under my jurisdiction." Suzanna stood her ground. "My criteria for deciding which wholesaler—"

Rutherford interrupted her explanation. "I don't care what your criteria is. We are not doing business in any shape, form or fashion with that man." He ended his declaration by clamping his teeth on the stubby cigar.

Suzanna breathed deeply to keep her voice under control. She didn't appreciate Rutherford's interference. If he hadn't been here today, she probably wouldn't even have discussed the issue with him. But she couldn't help wondering what would have happened if she'd gone ahead with her plan and Rutherford had discovered later that they were buying from Chase. It wasn't a comfortable feeling.

She tried to look confident. "I look for quality first, then price and convenience. Clearly Chase's products are superior in all three areas. Alec even admitted it."

"Suzanna, we'd better have a little talk about this."

"I'll be glad to show you my comparisons. Come on into my office."

Left without an alternative, Rutherford followed, puffing heavily on the cigar, blowing smoke everywhere.

Suzanna picked up a sheet of paper from her desk and handed it to him. "I think this is a valid consideration. You can see that—"

"Suzanna, listen to me." He ignored her comparison notes. "I don't care if Chase Clements is recommended by the Pope. We are not doing business with the man. I won't contribute to his trade."

"Even when it benefits us and our clients?"

"Not even." He let the paper float to her desk.

"Look, I know there's been bad blood between you two. But, can't you put that in the past? He's just a businessman, like any other."

"Oh, no. Chase Clements isn't like the rest of us."

No, she thought. He's himself. "Do you know him, Mr. Rutherford? He seems perfectly agreeable to work with us."

"Of course, he is. That man'll do anything to make me look bad. Who knows how he made his money?" Rutherford waved one hand. His pin-striped suit coat flapped open to reveal that he wore black suspenders. His pot belly hung over his waistband. "Clements might have a gambling operation hidden there, or maybe he's running a little whiskey on the river. He's over there by himself. No one knows what he's up to."

She wanted to shout *No he isn't! I've been over there!* but pressed her lips together. "Those are some pretty strong accusations, Mr. Rutherford. I think you're absolutely wrong about Clements." She took a seat at her desk and gripped the arms of her chair. It took all her willpower to keep her temper. This was her first real face-to-face confrontation with her boss, and it was a doozer. Could she handle him and his irrational reasoning, and keep her job?

Of course, she told herself calmly. She had to retain this job. She'd had difficult moments with employers before and managed to work through them. She reminded herself that professional managers could handle petty office problems. However, when Rutherford attacked Chase, she took offense and felt that she had to defend him from Rutherford's unfair suspicions. Anyway, he was wrong!

She cleared her throat. "You must know that Clements runs a legitimate business, or he'd be shut down by now."

"I don't know anything for a fact. I've never been to the Boon Docks, myself. I know he refused to sell the property. That means he has a good thing going over there on the river. And it's well-known that his father was always up to no good."

"Chase is not his father!" Suzanna could feel her voice rising. Self-control, she reminded herself. Self-control!

"Like father, like son."

"That isn't always true."

"He's a Clements, isn't he? The matter's closed, Suzanna. We won't buy one mud catfish from that man!"

"The new chef has some innovative recipes and wants to feature a daily fresh-fish house specialty. I think it's a good idea." Suzanna folded her arms in an effort to restrain her feelings. "Where would you suggest I go for the best products?"

"Try Newman's or one of those in Eureka Springs."

"Eureka Springs is nearly a hundred miles away! That isn't convenient. What about delivery?"

"I don't know. Ask McNeil. I trust his judgment."

"But not mine?"

"Look, Suzanna, I didn't say anything when I found out you'd hired a woman chef."

"What?" She was on her feet before she knew it. "You mean you object to the chef because she's a woman?"

"Now, don't go putting words in my mouth, Suzanna. Anyway, how was I to know that Kyle Hanes was a woman?"

"Mr. Rutherford—"

"Doing business with Clements goes too far. Now, just get it straight." He paused and listened. "I'm expecting a couple of the boys from the Rogues Club. I promised George Harlow and Daniel O'Hara I'd give them a tour of the place before lunch, and that sounds like them now. I do trust your judgment, Suzanna. Just keep that devious man, Clements, out of my business." Chomping on his smelly cigar, Rutherford lumbered away to greet his buddies.

Suzanna stood very still for a moment, listening to the men's jocular greetings. Finally she realized that her fists were clenched, as well as her stomach. Trying to cool down, she paced back and forth in her office. While she paced, she gave herself a pep talk about not risking her job and how endurance and patience would pay off for her and Ross.

She'd have to learn to overlook her boss's biases. Even as she was filled with a new determination to make this work, she thought about how everything involving Chase Clements was nothing but trouble.

And yet . . . she had no regrets.

She laced her fingers together and pressed them under her chin. Damn Rutherford, anyway! After his sexist comments about the female chef, she couldn't help wondering if she was a male manager, would he object so flatly to doing business with Chase? Or would the good-ole-buddy system kick in and allow them to do business for the sake of business, no matter what their personal feelings?

She quickly decided that Rutherford would have a fit about Chase, no matter who suggested it. The revelation didn't make her feel much better.

Suzanna knew that she could rationalize all day and, even though she was right, the bottom line was that Rutherford was boss, and she must comply with his wishes. Resigned, she walked to the window and looked out.

She could hear Rutherford and his cronies' laughter above the sounds of the carpenters in the kitchen. They were building extra storage space as a result of the new chef's recommendations. Kyle Hanes was going to be a good addition to the staff, and Suzanna was proud of hiring her. She would defend her choice of chef, if necessary.

Suzanna watched a man crossing the back lawn. As he approached the rear of the country club at the kitchen area, she narrowed her eyes and leaned forward. Something about him looked familiar. She shrugged it off, thinking he was probably one of the carpenters.

The man carried a shirt box in one hand. Curious, she gave him a closer inspection. Those long legs encased in tight, tight jeans. The purposeful way he walked. The front of his brown leather jacket, comfortably open to reveal a cinnamon turtleneck. That disheveled hair. Those dark sunglasses, boldly hiding drop-dead eyes.

She knew exactly who was coming—Chase Clements. What in the world was he doing here? Coming to see Rutherford? Unlikely. Then he must be here to see her. She thought of Rutherford and his cronies roaming around the club. So she dashed out and through the kitchen.

"Chase!" she confronted him in a loud whisper. "What do you want?"

He stood still and looked at her, a teasing grin on his tanned face. Slowly he removed his sunglasses. "You."

"I should have asked what you're doing here."

"Finding you."

"But why here? Don't you know Rutherford hates you?"

"I'm not here to see him. I'm here for you."

After her recent argument with her boss concerning Chase, Suzanna figured she'd better get him out of sight before Rutherford saw him. *Saw them together.* "Then let's go into my office."

She took his hand and hurried him through the kitchen and down the short hallway to her office. Once inside, she closed the door and breathed a sigh of relief. "Now." Suzanna folded her arms. "What is it?"

Chase grinned at her in that rakish, melt-your-heart way of his. "Are you ashamed of me, hiding me like this?"

"No, of course not."

"It's kind of fun, actually."

She shook her head. "Chase, don't you know it's risky for you to be here? Rutherford hates you so, he would probably explode if he knew you were here."

"Especially if he knew I was closed up in his manager's tiny office." He paused long enough to give her an approving once-over. "Alone with his very attractive employee." Chase gestured at her outfit. The casual matching slacks and tie-front blouse fitted her body with relaxed elegance. "You look fabulous in that color."

"Magenta."

"Looks like purple to me." He grinned. "Sets me on fire."

She tried not to show that she was on fire, too. "We, uh, Mr. Rutherford and I were just discussing you."

"Me?" He laughed. "Getting down and dirty, huh?"

"Chase, I'm very upset. I had intended to buy our fish from the Boon Docks. But Mr. Rutherford has a personal vendetta. He absolutely refuses."

"I'm not surprised."

"I'm furious."

"Because of me? Or because he refused your proposal?"

"Both, I guess." Chase had the remarkable ability to see through her.

"Don't worry about me. I'm not depending on the Rutherford Country Club to make my profits. Good thing, too."

"I tried to convince him, but he's adamant. You must have really made him mad."

"You either love me or hate me." He shrugged. "Most folks around here do the latter."

"Why?"

He shook his head. "They have set notions. I have an unsavory history here."

"Everybody's got a past. We've all made mistakes."

"But the big difference between you and me, Suzanna, is that I don't apologize for mine. Or my old man's. That's just the way it was, not necessarily the way it is now."

"I tried to explain that to Rutherford."

"Some folks can't tolerate bluntness. I tell it like it is, and they don't want to hear that. Rutherford has decided that I'm no good. And no one's going to change his mind."

"You're absolutely right." She shook her head. "I tried to reason with him, but there's no way. He's decided and that's that."

"Don't waste your time."

"You act as if you don't care."

"I don't care nearly as much as you do, Suz. 'Course it would have been nice to have such a lucrative contract as the country club's, but I never—ever—thought that anything Rutherford did would pad my pockets. I can live without Rutherford's business. Now, you, Suzanna. That's a different story."

"I like your honesty, Chase."

"You fluctuate between apologizing to the world for being you and being honest with me. Like now. When I tell you how I feel around you, you change the subject."

"You aren't talking about feelings. You're talking about your physical reactions."

"Thanks for clearing it up for me," he drawled with a little grin. "But, I sure feel that fire whenever I'm around you." He lifted the box and handed it to her. "Maybe this will say something about real feelings. Like regret about the cycle wreck."

"Chase . . ." She took the box reluctantly. "What's this?"

"Open it and see."

She read the name on the box, then looked at him questioningly. "O'Hara's?" Daniel O'Hara's elegant department store was the most expensive in the state of Arkansas. A purchase from O'Hara's meant big bucks.

"Open it," he encouraged, his face suddenly lit with boyish enthusiasm.

She sat at her desk and lifted the lid. Nestled in the gold-star-studded tissue paper was a blue sweater. It wasn't just any blue. This was the color of a fair, clear sapphire and very nearly the exact color of Suzanna's eyes. Lifting the garment, she knew it wasn't just any sweater. It was incredibly soft; the knit design, unbelievably precise. "Chase! It's an Erin Ennis from Ireland."

"If you're going after a sweater, why not go where they make the best?"

"But, Chase, sweaters imported from Ireland are terribly expensive."

He took the sweater by the shoulders and placed it on her chest. "Let's see how it looks. Yep, just about matches your eyes."

"Chase, I can't let you do this."

"Did I ask permission? It's done."

"This is too much."

"I'm just replacing the one I destroyed in the wreck."

"This is *not* replacing that sweater." She touched the item with loving strokes. "This one must have cost as much as my entire winter wardrobe."

He reached out and caressed her cheek in a gesture that was both tender and bold. "I'd like to see you in it. To see if it fits."

Suzanna's breath caught in her throat. The energy of his touch sent her senses reeling. Forgetting for the moment that they were at the country club and that she had hidden Chase behind her closed office door, she could only go along with his beckoning.

"I . . . I'll wear it next time I see you."

"Then, there will be a next time? You'll come back to the Boon Docks?" His dark eyes caressed her face while his hand trailed sensually down her neck.

She swallowed hard. "You seem to know I can't stay away."

"I only know that you don't leave my imagination, Suzanna. Ever." His fingertips reached the pulse point at the base of her neck and lingered. His lips hovered close to hers.

She could taste their sweet warmth before he even kissed her. And she didn't resist when he claimed her mouth in a searing kiss. She leaned into it, allowing— no—welcoming it. He pulled her to her feet and as she rose, his tongue dipped between her lips. Heat pounded through her breasts, creating tingling all the way to the tips.

His hands framed her body, sliding upward until they cupped her breasts. Softly his thumbs stroked the sensitive curves.

At the sound of someone coming down the hall to her office, they reluctantly broke apart.

"Oh, my God, Chase!" Suzanna whispered breathlessly as she gathered the sweater in her arms.

"Don't let on. Be cool." He stepped against the wall behind the door just as it opened.

Suzanna turned to greet her visitor, standing so that she blocked the view of the sweater and box on her desk.

Mr. Rutherford stuck his head in the door. "Suzanna, the boys and I are going to town for lunch. Won't it be nice when we can have it here?"

Still stunned by Chase's kiss, Suzanna struggled to sound somewhat intelligent. "Yes, sir."

"I'll see you tomorrow."

"Right."

"No more problems over the Clements issue?"

"No, sir. It's . . . over." Even as she spoke, she could see Chase standing against the wall. Nothing with him was over! What was she going to do?

"'Atta girl!"

Suzanna glared at the door after Rutherford had closed it. She could hear him join his cronies in the foyer. The front door slammed, and she knew he was gone. She looked at Chase.

"'Atta girl?" he mocked.

She turned away from his accusing gaze.

"Is that for doing his bidding, Suzanna?"

Angrily she shook her fist at the imaginary boss. "He's such a jerk!"

"Don't humiliate yourself like that, Suzanna."

She began to fold the sweater neatly in its box. "Don't you know that employees have to agree with employer, even if they think the boss is a jerk?"

"Do you have to kowtow?"

"I'm not kowtowing! I'm just—" She whirled around. "Oh, you wouldn't understand! *You* don't have to answer to anyone!"

He walked toward her slowly. "I have to answer to *me*, and I'm my own toughest judge."

"I'm not ashamed of making the effort to keep my job, Chase Clements." She propped her hands on her hips, and her eyes flashed. "I'm a single parent. I'm responsible for my son's well-being, his care and education. If Zack ever contributed a cent toward his son, I'd probably faint. Furthermore, it isn't easy for a woman to get a job in this one-horse town, much less one as good as the manager of a brand-new country club. Rutherford and I will work out our differences. It just takes time. And I don't need you to tell me how difficult Old Man Rutherford is!"

Chase backed away one step with both palms out. "Excuse me! You're right, Suzanna. You do have a lot of responsibility. But that part, I understand perfectly."

"There's a big difference between me and you, though, Chase. You have your own property and business. I have—" she gestured with one hand "—nothing!"

He moved to her and clasped her hand, pressing her palm to his. "You're right. I do have the river property. And I don't have any right to step in here and tell you what to do and how to do it." He moved closer and circled her waist with his other arm. "I'm well aware of the differences between us, Suzanna. I revel in them."

With the same boldness that he'd exhibited since she'd invaded his land, he kissed her. Hard, demandingly, erotically. His lips captured hers. His tongue plunged into her mouth, deeply and sensually. He pressed her full length to his hard, lean body. He let her know, in no uncertain terms, that he wanted her. But that wasn't surprising. He'd said as much from the first moment they met.

When he released her, Suzanna felt weak. She clung to his arms, not willing to admit what he did to her, yet not willing to give him up. She wanted him to stay, but feared what would happen if he did. She wanted more of his kisses, more of him. But she feared she would lose total control if she relaxed for a moment.

He kissed her again. Quickly, this time. "I don't have to elaborate on what you do to me, Suzanna."

"I'm not oblivious, Chase."

"I can tell you don't hate it when I kiss you."

"I . . . I fear it, though."

"You're afraid of me?"

"Not you. But of what might happen."

"Is that why you're going out with Alec this weekend?"

She raised her chin and replied. "Maybe."

Chase was direct, as usual. "I hope you have a miserable time with him. Still trying to fit the mold, huh, Suzanna?"

"What do you mean?"

"Trying to please. This time, I'll bet it's your mother. Is she very happy that you're going out with Alec McNeil?"

"Yes, but that's not why I'm going."

"Why, then?"

"He's a nice man, a perfect gentleman."

"Not like me at all, huh?"

"Chase," she chided, her eyes dancing with a little smile, "are you jealous?"

"Extremely."

"Don't be. This is simply a casual date."

"Good. Save the hot ones for me."

She laughed. "You are the boldest man I've ever known."

"Oh, Suz-anna . . ."

No one had ever simply spoken her name and made it sound sexy.

"Thanks for the sweater, Chase. It's beautiful."

"Will you wear it for me?"

"Yes."

"Just for me? If you get too bored Saturday night, come on over."

"Don't wait up." She chuckled as he slipped from their loose embrace.

Suzanna watched Chase striding across the back lawn. She admired that gait of his. Chin high, eyes straight ahead, he walked with no hesitation. He took long steps and swung his arms naturally. He didn't care, as she did, whether he was discovered on Rutherford's property. He was a free man—free to do and say as he damned-well pleased without thinking of upsetting anyone. And she envied him. She wished she could do the same. But the reality was that she had to keep her job, had to keep working for a jerk.

She watched as Chase straddled his motorcycle. He was sexy! Vividly she recalled the feeling of tucking her body next to his when they rode together. And she grew warm just thinking of his lean, muscular form moving with hers.

Quickly turning away, she covered her face with cold, clammy hands. She had to stop thinking of Chase this way.

Nothing was as easy as it seemed. Why couldn't she just move back to Grace, fall in love with some down-home guy and get married? That's what she really wanted—not an adventure with the town black sheep. That's why she had accepted this date with Alec. But she knew she dreaded every "nice" moment.

CHASE PULLED his pickup truck to a halt beneath the spreading arms of an elm tree. It was no accident that found him traveling by the back road that led past the duck pond and the ninth hole of Rutherford's golf course. In sight over the hill was Suzanna's cottage.

With a sullen expression, he watched Alec McNeil's Chevrolet pull in front of the cottage. Soon Suzanna and Ross hopped into the car with Alec and drove out of sight.

Chase gripped the steering wheel and pressed hard on the accelerator of the aged blue pickup. Everything about that woman ignited him. Thoughts of her set his mind aflame with erotic fantasies.

Pushing the old truck, he made a billowy cloud of dust on the dirt road. At the Boon Docks, he changed vehicles and rode the cycle into the woods—fast. He returned in a foul mood and snapped at everyone, including Bo.

"I thought you were going to reorganize the fishing-rod section in the front of the store, Bo."

"Yep. That's my intention." The big man lifted a case of soft drinks and moved them to the rear storage room. "Haven't had a chance to get to it."

"Well, if you'd utilize your time better, you could do it." Chase looked at Ken. "What are you staring at? You were supposed to clean the area around that worm farm of yours. Do I have to do everything around here?"

"I'll take care of it, Dad."

Bo gave Ken a sympathetic glance. "How would you like to come over to my house tonight, Ken, and help me make those fancy fishing lures?"

"Yeah, Bo!" Ken nodded enthusiastically. "Would you show me how?"

"Sure thing. I'm melting the lead and pouring them into molds tonight. While you're there, would you like to spend the night? Sunday I usually make pancakes."

"Great!"

"Is that okay with you, Chase?"

Chase responded with a little wave of his hand. "Sure. Go on."

Bo circled Ken's slim shoulders with his large arm and steered him out of the shop. "Come on, buddy. Let's get started. And leave your dad alone." He emphasized the last word and glared at Chase.

Chase ignored him. He knew he was being an ass. And the best thing they could do for him was to get out of his way.

"Want to come over in the morning for pancakes, Dad?" Ken offered.

"No, I, uh—" Chase stopped and reconsidered. The boy kept trying. "Sure, Ken."

"Okay! See you in the morning, Dad." Ken turned to Bo as they headed out the door. "Do you still have that blueberry syrup, Bo?"

Chase was glad to be alone in his misery. He entertained himself with a beer and watching boxing on TV.

He didn't particularly care about either. But he couldn't enjoy anything for thinking of one gray-eyed, dark-haired, very sexy lady who was spending the evening in another man's company.

6

CHASE GLANCED AT his digital watch. After midnight. He stood by the living-room window and watched the two headlights travel the old road into the Boon Docks compound. He could tell they belonged to a compact car, coming from the direction of Rutherford's property.

The lights passed the main buildings and veered onto the dirt road leading to the cabins. They moved steadily to the end of the row, turned into his driveway and halted. Even before the car door opened, he knew it was Suzanna.

He waited for her in the open doorway.

Suzanna saw his shadowed form when she stepped onto the porch. He stood with his legs apart and one hand was hooked casually to the doorframe above his head. The man was formidable and at the same time irresistible. Was she asking for problems or was she merely a fool?

Watching him, she stubbed her toe on the top step. It was a bold move, not well-thought-out—coming here in the middle of the night, seeking Chase. "I hope I didn't wake you, Chase."

"I couldn't sleep." He moved back so she could enter. They stood silently for a moment in the semidark room. Chase forced himself to inquire, "How was your evening with Alec?"

"Fine. Alec is very nice."

"'Nice' is boring."

"'Nice' is steady and upstanding."

"Not like me?"

"You're all those things, Chase. And . . . more."

"More?" He laughed, soft and low. "Or less?"

"Don't underestimate yourself."

"Oh, I don't. But I realize that I'm not at all like Alec McNeil."

She studied Chase in the darkness. "No, as a matter of fact, you aren't. Does that bother you?"

"Not one bit. Unless he's the kind of man you're looking for. You see, I know where I stand with the town. It's where I stand with you, though, that really matters to me."

She didn't want to admit that Alec McNeil was indeed the kind of man she had in mind, if she should consider *any* man. But she couldn't stay away from Chase. "Does it, Chase? I thought you didn't care what anyone thought."

"Only you. Actually, I'm more concerned about feelings. How you feel when you're with me." He shifted closer. "What about when you and Alec are together? Any sparks?"

"We . . . we got along fine." Chase's fragrance—a warm, sexy, moss aroma—seemed to embody his magnetic power over her. She wondered if he'd applied it purposely. Could he have known she'd come tonight? How could he? She didn't know it, herself, until just a few minutes ago.

"No fire?" His body loomed near, strong and imposing. Intimidating. Beguiling. Wildly exciting.

This was what Chase meant. Trying to imagine experiencing this driving compulsion with Alec, Suzanna let out a soft laugh. "Not a flicker."

"That's all I need to know." He moved forward, gripping her arms and hauling her to him. "Suzanna . . ." he murmured in that Southern way of his.

Suzanna wanted his kiss; had dreamed about it; couldn't sleep tonight for thinking about it. She knew he wouldn't disappoint her.

His lips came down on hers with fierce passion. They moved as if to devour her with a desperate hunger. Suzanna's mouth opened to allow the sweet probing they both desired. Their tongues met, parried, then stroked to sweeter depths. This was what she'd been waiting for all evening, all week, since the last kiss. She was addicted to his responses, excited by the promise of his passion, and in that heat-crazed moment, wanted him more than anything. Or anyone.

He wrapped his arms around her, caressing her back with large, sure hands, molding her to him. She felt the power of his body and wanted more. Much more.

Obsessed with satisfying her passionate yearning, Suzanna feared that the only way was to be fulfilled by the sexual prowess of the man who held her. She was starved for the fierce, hard lovemaking Chase promised in his every glance, his every movement.

But a small voice inside her warned her: *Slow down. This man is trouble.*

She forced her hands between their clinging bodies. Through his shirt, she could feel him warm and taut. She touched the hard, round buttons of his nipples and let her hands slide over his chest. All she could think of was the sensual pleasure of exploring that bare, masculine expanse. Her hands itched to know him more.

Meanwhile his lips ventured to make a cool, moist trail down her neck and under one ear.

"Chase—" she managed.

"Umm, you're delicious." He tickled her earlobe with his tongue.

"Chase, slow down." Suzanna struggled for control of her own senses.

"This is why you came tonight."

"No! I...I came to show you the sweater." It was only half a lie.

He straightened and drew a long breath.

She could feel his pounding heartbeat, hear his heavy breathing. He remained holding her, silently, and she wondered what he was thinking—how he must despise her at the moment. "Don't hate me for this, Chase. I don't know why I came. Ross is spending the night at Mama's. And I was alone."

"You know why you came."

"No...I—"

"You just don't want to admit it, Suz." He loosened his grip on her slightly. "It's okay. I'm alone, too. Ken is at Bo's."

Her heart accelerated at the thought that they were alone in the house with nothing or no one to stop them. "Maybe I shouldn't be here."

"You're crazy if you think I'll let you leave now."

With that warning, she should have been apprehensive. But this was Chase. She had no fear of him or what the night might hold. "Am I your prisoner?" Her voice was teasing.

"I won't force anything on you, Suz." One hand came around to touch her chin. "You'll come of your own accord. You have so far, haven't you?"

She couldn't deny the truth. "Yes."

He reached down and switched on the table lamp. "Let's see how the sweater fits."

She blinked at him. The light was low but still more than her pupils were used to. It took her eyes a moment to adjust. He wore a gunmetal-gray sport shirt tucked into black jeans. The shirt was of finely woven corduroy and as smooth and soft as butter beneath her fingers—a contrast to the tantalizing ruggedness of muscle and brawn beneath it.

He looked mysterious . . . almost dangerous. Chase was the kind of man she couldn't resist. And exactly what she must.

He opened her jacket and slid it off her shoulders. The pale sapphire sweater fit her with a well-worn familiarity. Its mock turtleneck was loose around her throat and the front panel of luxuriously textured knit separated the gentle swells of her breasts in a provocative way. Chase was intrigued with the intimacy with which the garment hugged her body.

"Nice."

"Is that all you can say?" She modeled for him, pirouetting with one arm along her thigh, the other bent with her hand on her hip.

"No, that isn't all I *can* say. But it's probably all I *should* say."

"Say it," she taunted.

He ignored her challenge and resisted the impulse to strip the gorgeous sweater from her tempting body. "Do you like it?"

"I love it. Do you?"

"Oh, yes."

"It feels—" she groped for the right word "—extravagant. Maybe it's because I know it must have cost you a chunk. Anyway, it's far better than the sweater I tore in the wreck. Thank you, Chase."

"My pleasure. I'm a little surprised you came over to show me."

"Didn't you expect it?"

"Hoped. Let's sit by the fire." He gestured. "Would you like a beer?"

"I'd rather have something hot. Chocolate?"

"How about Kahlua chocolate?"

"Perfect."

"I'll be right back."

Suzanna nestled on the sofa in front of the fireplace. A few remaining coals glowed softly.

Chase brought steaming mugs of hot chocolate liberally laced with Kahlua and topped with a dollop of whipped cream. He stooped to add a cedar log to the fire, and she marveled at the lines of his body. She relished the ripple of muscles across his back and the power evident in his arms as he stoked the blaze. Again she admired the way his jeans stretched tight around his firm thighs. And she imagined those thighs surrounding hers.

He moved to the stereo. "What kind of music would you like? Cool blues? What about old-time jazz? I have a fine new album of Coleman Hawkins greats."

"I love jazz. But I thought country music was more your style."

"Not entirely." He joined her on the sofa as the mellow sounds of the tenor sax played low. "Even though his heyday was in the thirties, Hawkins is still the standard for jazz tenors. This album's called *Body and Soul*. Like it?"

"Very much." Suzanna studied the fire and sipped her hot chocolate. Chase continually caught her off guard. Just when she thought she had him pegged, he showed her that he was different. The music seemed appropriate for the evening. The album title seemed to express exactly the way Chase had captured Suzanna; *body and soul.*

At his encouragement, she chatted about her evening out. However, she was careful to avoid any mention of her escort, Alec.

Chase relaxed beside her on the sofa. The hour was late, the drink, extremely soothing; the music, like an erotic perfume, filtering and drifting. Suzanna was, as always, irresistible. She sat beside him, her slender, usually tense body relaxed. Her face reflected a soft, silky glow in the firelight. She was where she belonged now—with him. They could be honest with each other. Trust each other. Before he realized it, Chase was discussing a dream that he'd never revealed to anyone except Bo. "For years now, I've wanted to build additions to the Boon Docks."

"What's stopped you?"

"Lack of sufficient funds. And Rutherford."

"How Rutherford?"

"When he tried to buy me out and I refused, he vowed to ruin me. What he meant was that he'd keep the business community from supporting me."

"How can he do that?"

"He's mighty influential around these parts. I'm not. In fact, the banks have refused to loan me money for improvements or additions to my business."

"On what grounds?"

"That my assets aren't substantial and stable enough." He shrugged. "It angers me that Rutherford can borrow and do whatever he wants with his property, but I can't do the same with mine."

"You can't borrow from any bank around here?"

"I'd have to go out of town. Until recently I didn't have the assets to do that."

"Essentially, then, he's stopped your progress." Suzanna could sympathize with Chase's dissatisfaction. No wonder he and Rutherford were such fixed enemies. Their conflicts went far and deep.

"He's slowed me down, not stopped me. What I've done has been on profits alone. Now it looks like we have enough to seriously consider expanding—no thanks to Rutherford or the community. Most of our business is statewide, like the wholesale fish trade. Some goes beyond state boundaries. Many of the guests who rent our cottages are from out of state."

"What do you want to add? More cottages?"

He shook his head. "A fleet of boats to be used for float fishing. And maybe someday, a restaurant on the hill overlooking the river."

"That's near Rutherford's property." It was the area he'd shown her that day on the motorcycle. "Overlooking the old pecan grove?"

"Now it's the ninth hole. It's one of the reasons I refused to sell to him. Although I certainly could have used the money, dreams can't be bought. The other reason I would never sell to Rutherford or anyone else is that this property may be the only asset I leave my son. But it'll be his."

She pressed his hand, which lay on the sofa between them. "You're quite different from the man the town views you as, Chase. And from the one I originally thought you were."

"And what was that? A hell-raiser?"

"Sort of."

"One who never stayed home at night, thinking about a woman who was out with another man?"

"You didn't go to hear your bluegrass group tonight?"

"I wasn't in the mood." He slid his arm around her shoulder. "I told you, Suzanna, you've captured me. You won't leave my mind . . . my imagination." He teased her ear with his tongue.

Her heart pounded with renewed desire and hope. Chase was admitting that he was preoccupied by her, rather than making his usual arrogant boast that she couldn't stay away from him. Was he telling the truth? Had she known him to lie or deceive? If nothing else, she had to trust him. "Then, that makes two of us, Chase."

He caressed her face softly with feather-light fingertips. "At night I dream of touching you, Suzanna." He planted small kisses along her cheek. "Caressing, exploring, touching you everywhere." His hand dropped beneath her chin to her neck. His fingers circled it and moved around to the back. Slowly he lowered his head to hers.

This time his lips gently urged hers to open. His tongue slid between her teeth to tantalize her soft mouth. She closed over it, creating a gentle sucking motion, and felt the effect swirling through her veins. Suddenly she was hot—hot for him.

And he knew it.

He aligned them on the sofa, covering her with his hard body. Reaching beneath her sweater, he spread his fingers around her rib cage as he straightened her under him, molding them together sensually. His hands encountered the warm swells of her breasts and he began to caress them. Suzanna sighed and arched upward.

She felt him release her bra. His hands were in direct contact with her flesh, gently massaging, teasing her tightening nipples until she moaned aloud.

"Suz, so smooth . . . everything I imagined."

"Hold me, Chase. Love me. . . ."

"Come with me, Suz-anna," he drawled in a low voice. "To my bed. I'll love you like you've never been loved before."

She allowed Chase to pull her to her feet and whisk her into the cool quarters of his bedroom. He closed the door and motioned her onto the quilted bed. She sat on the edge and began pulling off her socks. By the time he came toward her, he was already half undressed.

His chest with its sandy layer of hair seemed broader in the dim light of the bedroom, especially when she knew that chest would soon be crushing hers. When he stripped off his jeans, she could think of nothing but that his body would soon possess her. She'd never been so excited. Nor so anxious.

With impatient hands he helped her finish removing her clothes. The sweater and bra were quickly discarded. Then, her slacks and panties. In one motion, he ran his hands up her outer thighs to her waist and slid her onto the bed. He stood there for a moment, looking at her, devouring her with his eyes. "Suzanna, are you protected?"

"I, uh . . ." She stared back, distracted by the compelling sight of him. "No, I didn't expect—"

"Then I'll take care of it." He disappeared into the bathroom briefly before lowering himself to the bed beside her. "I can't believe you're actually here. It's been my fantasy to have you in my bed since I first saw you."

"Your fantasy is to have me here, in your bed? That isn't very imaginative." She let her hand trail across his chest.

He stroked the soft mounds of her breasts. "I'm a very basic guy," he murmured. "I don't need exotic locales when touching you here drives me wild."

"Me, too." She bowed her back as his tantalizing hand moved down her torso. "It's wild enough for me to be in your bed tonight, Chase." She moaned as his hand slid between her legs.

He caressed the heart of her until she opened to him. "I want you, Suz. Like this." He moved over her, his chest crushing hers, just as she had imagined it. His strong thighs wedged between hers. His erection teased her sensitive skin.

She reached down and grasped him, guiding him to her.

Chase groaned aloud.

"Yes," she whispered. "Like this. Now."

He nestled in her thighs, and the heat of his aroused body spread over her.

In that moment when their flesh met, Suzanna knew that she had waited all her life for this—for him. And this glory was her reward for coming back home. Chase was everything she had looked for, and failed to find in Zack—only much more.

She tried to savor each inch of him as he advanced. But Chase had no more patience for savoring. He had to have her. Now. He entered her with a series of hard thrusts. She cried out with the intense, mounting pleasure and gripped the pillow beneath her head with both fists.

"Come with me, Suz." His urgency increased as he lifted her hips and pushed deeper.

"Wait for me." She felt herself slipping out of control as his pulsing cadence began. Suddenly the throbbing she felt was transformed into vigorous ripples of pleasure purling through her. With her head back and her mouth open, she let him take her completely as she exploded into a glorious climax.

Uttering a harsh groan, he shuddered with one final thrust and collapsed over her. They lay very still for a long time, trying to prolong the ecstasy they had shared.

Then they slipped apart and folded together in an entwining embrace. He pulled the quilt over them, and they slept.

Sometime before daylight, Suzanna awoke. It took her a moment to realize that she was in a strange bed; and that the man beside her was—oh, Lord!—Chase Clements. She also realized that she had never been loved so thoroughly.

Chagrined, she remembered that she had come to him. Why, oh why, had she done such an aggressive thing? She glanced at him, then knew. Even in his sleep-tousled state, he was devastatingly handsome and utterly irresistible.

Well, now she *must* resist. And she *must not* let this happen again.

Slipping from the bed, she began to gather her clothes. They were scattered across the room. She struggled into each item as she found it. Pulling the beautiful blue sweater over bare breasts, she glanced back at Chase. Expecting him to be sleeping, she was astonished to find him staring at her. His eyes captivated her in the room's dim morning light.

"You don't have to go," he said quietly.

"Yes, I do." She found her other sock and hopped around as she put it on. "I shouldn't have stayed."

"Regrets already?"

"No, not about—" She looked up guiltily. "I have obligations. So do you. This isn't right for either of us. We have to forget. Make sure it doesn't happen again."

"Forget?" He laughed roughly. "I could never forget, Suz. And never want to."

"You have to." She swallowed hard and grabbed her slacks. "Because this is it. First and last time."

"I'd be willing to bet a million bucks you won't forget how you felt, either."

She sucked in a sharp breath. "Don't put your money where your mouth is, Chase. You'd lose." She whirled around and left the bedroom, grabbing her jacket from the living-room floor on the way out.

As she drove away in the morning mist, Suzanna admitted that she had been awfully rough on him—when it was herself that she was really angry with for having given in to her passion for Chase. Chase Clements was not the man for her, and she had to stay away from him.

A few hours later, she drove to her mother's to pick up Ross. She wondered if the guilt she felt showed in her face.

Ross met her at the door. "Hi, Mom! Come on in and speak on Gramma's tape recorder! She's using it in her new business!"

Suzanna followed Ross to the kitchen and kissed her mother on the cheek. "What's going on, Mama? What are you up to now?"

"Oh, I've been letting Ross play with the recorder. Listen." She beamed as the sound of Ross's young voice rose proudly from the little machine on the table! "We've been having fun."

"I'm glad." Suzanna smiled at her mother in return. She was happy to see that the two had patched up their differences of last week with something of mutual interest. She laughed as she listened to the recordings Ross and her mother had made. At their encouragement, she contributed her own words to the family tape.

When Ross grew tired of it, he wandered away. Suzanna turned to her mother. "What's it for? What business?"

"Oh, it's not really a business. It's just a little project I'm doing." Ellie changed the tape. "Actually, the idea came from you, Suzanna."

"Me? What in the world?"

Ellie's face shone with pleasure as she explained. "Well, I thought about what you'd said about the library committee's county history project—that the real history is in the facts behind the gossip we Crazy Quilters exchange . . . that happenings in people's lives are the most interesting things. So I talked with Mary Ellen Walsh, who's in charge of putting the library project together. And I volunteered to record oral histories from some of our older residents."

"Mama, that's wonderful! What a great idea! And a good thing to do for the community."

"Now . . ." Ellie sat on the edge of the chair opposite Suzanna. "Tell me about last night."

Suzanna's mouth flew open. "Wh-what?" How could her mother know? And why was she smiling like that?

"Come on, sugar, you can tell your mama. How was it?"

"Uh—" Suzanna's mind whirled. There was no way she could tell her mother about last night. She hadn't even planned on admitting to having seen Chase.

"You two looked so charming driving off together in that beautiful car of his. Was he a gentleman? Are you going to see him again?"

Suzanna felt giddy with relief. Her mother was talking about her date with Alec, not the night she'd spent with Chase! She giggled impulsively. "Oh, Mama, Alec was the perfect gentleman. We had a very nice time."

"I knew it!" Ellie beamed happily, her blue eyes shining. "He's really a good man, Suzanna. Everyone likes and respects Alec McNeil. He has such good standing in the community."

Ellie's words stabbed home, and Suzanna reflected how totally unlike Alec Chase was. And how Rutherford had made good his vow to ruin Chase's already poor standing in the community.

From the rapt expression on her mother's face, Suzanna realized that her feigned response to the evening with Alec had been too enthusiastic. Ellie had mistaken Suzanna's relief for delight over Alec. But she didn't have the heart to burst Ellie's bubble. Certainly her mother would have been horrified to know that she'd left Alec's company for Chase Clements's bed. And in retrospect, even Suzanna couldn't believe she'd done it.

"Alec is very nice when we're alone."

Ellie clasped her hands to her heart. "He could be very good for you and Ross."

Suzanna shuddered at the thought and changed the subject. "So, Mama, when do you start with this wonderful new project of yours?"

Ellie smiled knowingly and patted her daughter's hand. "You don't want to talk about it, do you, dear? I understand how you want to keep some things private."

"Well, it was just a first date. There isn't much to tell." There'd been nothing—and especially, no sparks. Now, with Chase—

"It's okay to have a few secrets, Suzanna. Really."

"I don't have secrets, Mama." Oh, dear, it was getting worse! She had a huge secret that she couldn't tell anyone! "Please, Mama, tell me more about your project."

"Well, I've already made my first tape. I spent two hours with Alberta Hemstead, talking about how she grew up on Hanke's Ridge and what life was like before they paved the road and it became an elite residential area." Ellie grinned proudly. "Want to hear it?"

"Yes. Oh my, yes!" Suzanna was anxious to talk and think about anything other than Chase.

7

By November Suzanna was beginning to feel a degree of satisfaction with her new life. Ross had adjusted well to the new school and was making friends. His participation in the after-school sports program was proving to be good for him in many ways.

Her mother was starting to branch out, making her historical recordings with a zeal that Suzanna hadn't thought was possible anymore. Everyone noticed that there was a lively new sparkle in Ellie's eyes these days.

Suzanna's job was rocking along. The Rutherford Country Club was due to open in a matter of weeks. With the remodeling complete, the carpenters had gone. Suzanna appreciated the quiet in her office and the absence of their constant hammering and loud radios in the background.

Idly she fingered the carpet swatches on her desk. The decorators would be here soon. Actually, she was a little surprised that Mr. Rutherford had asked for her input on the interior decorating. But then, Rutherford had a way of surprising her occasionally.

Her mind wandered, as it often did, to Chase. And she couldn't help smiling. Everyone and everything was moving in a respectable, forward direction—except Suzanna's personal life.

Oh, she had tried, really she had. But Alec McNeil simply was not her type of man. She suspected he realized it, too. But her mother didn't seem to notice. Ellie still had hopes that her only daughter would "marry right," and Alec was about as "right" as you could get in Grace. Instead, though, Suzanna had been meeting Chase Clements in secret.

"Suzanna! We have to talk! Immediately!"

She looked up with a start. Old Man Rutherford's cigar smoke preceded him into her office. "Sure. What's wrong, Mr. Rutherford?"

"Nothing's wrong! Things are going just right!" He grinned. "Wait'll you hear what's happened."

"Must be great." She was learning that the things that excited Old Man Rutherford rarely excited her.

"The opportunity, my dear. The opportunity for greatness!" He sat down in the Victorian chair next to her desk. "The Rogues Club has agreed to hold its next meeting here!"

"When is it?" She frowned. "We aren't quite ready to open yet."

"It'll be next week. We can be ready for a simple lunch meeting by then, can't we?"

Was there such a thing as a "simple lunch" for such a group? she wondered. "Well, I suppose we could push it, just for a luncheon."

"I want you to make whatever adjustments are necessary to accommodate this. It's very important, Suzanna. The Rogues have been talking about finding a better meeting place than the old Harness Hotel for a long time. Well, it's finally happened. Something in the heating system exploded and ruined our room. The walls and carpet are a mess. So, we have to do something fast. That's why I volunteered the country club."

"Hmm." Suzanna nodded. "So it's a case of taking advantage of a crisis situation."

"Right. 'Strike while the iron is hot,' my daddy always said. Why, depending on how much we impress them, we might become the permanent meeting place of the Rogues." He chuckled, obviously pleased with himself. "And I intend to impress them with the Rutherford Country Club."

"We'll do the best we can, under the circumstances."

"It's time for a little class for the Rogues. I tell you, it would be quite a coup if I could get them to meet here regularly." He propped his chubby hand on one broad knee. Smoke curled from the cigar, filling her office with its strong odor. "You know what this means, don't you, Suzanna?"

Money, she thought, but asked diplomatically, "In what way?"

"Simple logic, my dear. Most of the influential people in town, including the mayor, will be coming out here on a regular basis. Habits develop more habits. If they're constantly out here, it'll put pressure on them to join. Also, their families will want to get involved in the activities that'll be available here. It'll have a snowball effect."

"Yes, I suppose it will be good for business." Suzanna flipped to a clean sheet on her pad and began making notes. "We could try to finish the dining room first. Then, the foyer and central room."

"Right. I knew you'd be able to organize it for us, Suzanna." He puffed on his cigar. "I want this event to be perfect. The boys are naturally curious about the country club. We'll probably have our biggest turnout since that Japanese fellow came to talk about the new car plant they built a few years ago."

Suzanna smiled vaguely at his use of the word *boys* for the over-forty membership. She'd have to look after a million details, from the decor to hiring enough staff to pull off an elegant lunch. "How many will be attending? And what kind of meat choices do they want? And—"

He lifted the hand holding the cigar. "Charles Holbrooke is in charge of that. I'll have him contact you this week with details."

"Okay."

"You understand, Suzanna, that this is very important to me. I can see it now: The Rutherford Country Club, Home Of The Rogues Club."

"Yes, sir." She continued jotting notes to herself.

Rutherford walked to the door, then turned around for one last addendum. "Incidentally, Suzanna, this would be an excellent opportunity to give them a formal pitch about the country club. Could you prepare that?"

She blinked. "A speech?"

"Well, just a little rundown of what the country club offers and about your job here and, of course, how they can join."

"Sure," she said weakly. "I'd . . . be glad to."

"Do we have those membership applications from the printer's yet?"

"No. But I'll see if we can rush the order."

"'Atta girl."

She cringed and was glad Chase wasn't here to witness another embarrassing put-down.

"I knew you'd come through, Suzanna. This is going to be great. Just great." He walked down the hall muttering aloud about greatness.

Suzanna took a deep breath and let it out heavily. She looked down at her half page of notes. After the last line, she added, "Make A Speech! Great!" in big letters. Not only did she have to make sure the place was ready to receive guests in a week—when there was three weeks' work yet to be done—but she had to make a speech to boot!

"MAMA, HAVE YOU HAD your hair cut?" Suzanna hugged Ellie and welcomed her into the cottage.

"Oh, just had it trimmed a little. Do you like it?"

"I love it!" Suzanna made a big to-do over her mother's new hairstyle. It was another sign of change. Gone was the tight knot of hair on the back of Ellie's neck, and in its place was a perky cap of curls. "You look younger, Mama."

"Oh, go on, Suzanna!" Ellie giggled delightedly as she placed her grocery bag to the back of the kitchen counter. "Now, how can I help with supper?"

Suzanna gestured at the pot of boiling water on the stove. "The rice. I always get it too sticky. I'm doing the salad."

"That's because you stir it too much." Ellie started the rice, then casually asked, "When have you seen Alec lately?"

"I haven't had a chance, Mama. Been too busy." Suzanna changed the subject, launching into her exhausting efforts to accommodate Rutherford's demands for the Rogues Club luncheon.

Ellie was impressed, not so much with Suzanna's overtime as with the prospective guests. "The Rogues? Wonderful! Ah, Suzanna, you're starting off with the crème de la crème of Grace!" She nodded her approval and stirred the pot of rice once through before replacing the lid.

"At this point, I don't care who they are," Suzanna groaned, and furiously chopped celery for the salad. "Nobody is worth the stress caused by all this rushing to finish."

"Maybe the Rogues are. Alec is a member." Ellie gave her daughter a reproving nod. "They're the wealthy, powerful men in this town."

"Obviously Old Man Rutherford thinks so."

"Suzanna, you'd better stop calling him that. One of these days, you're going to slip up and say it to his face. Then you'll be sorry."

"You're right, Mama." Suzanna got the plates down, then reached for a glass. "But he's so impossible! The meeting's next week! The wallpaper isn't on the dining room yet, and the carpet isn't laid. I've called to rush it, but they have several jobs ahead of us. The wallpaper hasn't arrived from the supplier yet. And the carpet company can't possibly get to us before Tuesday of next week. The meeting's Thursday."

Ellie patted her daughter's hand. "You can do it, sugar. And if it isn't done, you'll do the best you can."

Suzanna gave her mother a weary look. "And to top it off, I'm supposed to give a sales pitch about the country club and all its assets, along with the different types of memberships."

"Sugar, talking's never has been a problem for you." She set the table for three.

"Talking's one thing. But this is a presentation to over seventy-five of the city fathers, including the mayor."

"I'll be so proud of you, sugar. Wish I could be there to hear it." She paused and looked wistful. "It would be the perfect opportunity to talk to Mr. O'Hara about Wordsworth, too."

"Who? About what?"

"Wordsworth. That's what we've decided to call the oral histories I'm recording. Isn't that neat?"

"Neat, Mama?" Suzanna couldn't believe this was her old-fashioned mother using such a contemporary term. She poured a glass of milk for Ross. "Wordsworth is a very clever name. I like it. Do you know Mr. O'Hara?"

Ellie nibbled a radish from the salad. "Not really. But I've been trying to contact him about doing a tape for us about the origins of O'Hara's Department Store. I know that his father and uncle started it around the turn of the century. But I'll bet he could give us some nice details for our histories."

"Probably could." Suzanna filled two coffee cups and set them on the table.

"So, that's why I want to talk to him. If you would arrange it so I could get in, I could hear you give your speech and see him at the same time."

Suzanna halted and looked at her mother. "Isn't the Rogues Club all-male?"

"Supposed to be."

"Well, I'm sure I'm not going to change that, Mama. How could I get you in there? I have instructions to make sure that even the waiters are male."

"Come on, Suzanna. Surely you could do something to help me." Ellie gave Suzanna a cajoling look.

"I'd love to, Mama, but . . ." She shook her head hopelessly.

Ellie propped her chin on the palm of her hand. "I've reached the end of my rope with trying to talk to that man."

"You can't get to him at his office?"

"I made an appointment with him, but when I got there, he'd canceled without even notifying me. After that, I left several messages with his secretary, but he hasn't returned my calls. He probably doesn't know what Wordsworth is. Anyway, I'm sure his secretary told him I was 'a little ole lady.'"

"That must have been before you got your hair cut, Mama."

Ellie grinned and fluffed her hair. "I'll bet he figures I want a contribution to the annual church auction or something."

Suzanna felt a little annoyed that such a powerful man would treat her mother so disrespectfully. "So, there must be another way."

"For the life of me, I can't think of any." Ellie sighed.

"You could try his office again."

"And again and again!" Ellie shook her head and hesitated. "I sure would appreciate a little help from my daughter who's in a position to make things happen."

"But, Mama, I'm not, really."

"You're going to be in the dining room with him, aren't you?"

"Not the whole time. Just for the speech."

"Which I'd like to hear."

Suzanna dumped the rice into a serving bowl. "I can't promise anything."

"Don't disappoint me, Suzanna," Ellie pleaded. "You won't have to do anything. Just let me in. I'll pretend I don't even know you."

Suzanna propped her hands on her hips. "Well, it shouldn't take long for you to speak to him."

Ellie answered enthusiastically. "I'd be very quick. I wouldn't disturb a soul."

"Oh, Mama, I know you won't," Suzanna assured her. "I think a brief meeting could be arranged."

"I knew I could rely on you, sugar!" Ellie hugged her daughter tightly and kissed her. "You won't have to do a thing. I promise!"

Suzanna moved to the table with the salad bowl. "Can we eat now, before you come up with another wild idea for Wordsworth? Where's the chicken you promised to bring?"

"In that brown paper sack. Could I have a platter?" Ellie asked innocently.

Suzanna watched curiously as her mother selected individual pieces of chicken from the large brown bag and placed them on the platter. "Mama, what are you doing?"

"Shh, don't say a word. I picked it up on the way over here."

"Colonel Sanders? I can't believe it!" Suzanna slapped her forehead. "I thought I'd never see the day when you bought fried chicken. It was always your pride and joy to cook it yourself."

Ellie lifted her eyebrows. "Times change, Suzanna. Get with it. I was too busy to cook today."

"You've changed a lot, Mama. A lot." Suzanna called Ross to dinner.

Ross scrambled noisily into the kitchen. "I'm starved! Hi, Gramma." He halted and gazed at her. "What did you do to your hair?"

Ellie looked up at her grandson, pleased that he'd noticed.

Suzanna held her breath. Oh, please don't say the wrong thing! She knew you could never tell with kids. And Ross wasn't always the most diplomatic person.

"You don't think it's too much?" Ellie asked with trepidation.

"I think it's *you*, Gramma. Only better!" He turned his attention to the table. "What's for supper? Fried chicken? Great! My favorite!"

Ellie beamed and shoved the platter of chicken toward her grandson. "I knew you liked it, Ross."

Suzanna let out a sigh of relief. She'd have to tell Ross later how good he'd made his grandmother feel and how proud she was of him. But as she joined her mother and son at the table, she could see that he knew it.

THE ROAR of a motorcycle penetrated the peace and quiet, but Suzanna didn't mind. She knew it meant Chase was coming. Their meetings by the river weren't exactly regular, but they happened often enough to be called frequent. She liked to come back to this familiar spot on the river. It was a good place to think, a private place to meet a friend. Which is what they'd become. Friends.

First, lovers. Then, friends. Usually it was the other way around. Friends became lovers. But not them. No, no. Suzanna and Chase had to be different. They had to give in to their instant physical attraction, then realize they liked to talk and joke and share.

They never mentioned that night Suzanna had slipped over to his house. *To his bed.* It had been a bold thing to do, and both attributed it to a need to give in to lust. Still, neither wanted to admit that there was anything more to their relationship than physical attraction. And friendship.

Suzanna smiled a welcome as Chase heaved down on the grassy spot beside her. He'd turned his brown leather jacket collar up against the cool breeze, and it framed his angular face. With shoulders hunched and hair tossed by the wind, he was, as always, ruggedly handsome. Everything about Chase, from the tough-casual way he dressed, to the aggressive way he'd made love to her was extremely masculine. No wonder she'd succumbed.

Chase didn't kiss her in greeting or touch her in any way, although he wanted to. His dark eyes said so. He just looked at her with longing. What he would have liked to do was whisk her away and kiss her until those gorgeous blue-gray eyes danced with joy, then ravage her body with loving.

He managed to keep his voice controlled. "I saw Ross fishing with Ken and figured you'd be here."

"Are they catching anything?"

"No. Too cold. But I didn't have the heart to tell them."

"Thanks for bringing Ross home from after-school sports yesterday."

Chase nodded. "Any time." He picked up a piece of dry grass and methodically broke it into inch-size pieces. "You've been working late every night this week."

"I have to. We have a group coming next week for a pre-opening lunch. There are a million things to do."

"Why rush it? If the place isn't ready, it isn't ready."

"Mr. Rutherford wants to try to entice the group to meet there regularly. It'll mean lots of business for the country club. Good PR. Promotion within the community. Regular customers. All that and more. He's right, too. It's good business."

"What group is it?"

"The Rogues Club."

Chase threw his head back and laughed. "Rutherford's bunch."

"Yes, I'm sure he's a member."

"I *know* he's a member of the Rogues." Chase tossed a small pebble into the water. "He and his elite bunch of cronies run the town."

"I suppose."

Chase's voice grew low and harsh. "They grease each other's wheels and keep things happening. They also *keep* things from happening."

She looked at him. His lips were pressed together tightly. "They're the ones who've kept you from getting loans?" she asked.

"Every bank president in town is a member. Oh, they're a close-knit group, the Rogues."

"I can understand why you despise them, Chase." She touched his hand, then slid hers into the warm confines of his.

"Actually, I don't despise them, Suz. It doesn't matter to me what they do anymore. I don't need them. And I don't care whether they approve of me or not." He angled his head at her. "But it should bother you. They're an elitist, all-male, sexist group."

"Of course. And I'm opposed to that. But there's nothing I can do about it."

"So, you're working day and night to get ready for them, making accommodations for this privileged group to gather regularly for a meeting you'd be excluded from merely because you're female? Doesn't make sense."

"Look, it's my job to do that. Apparently, nothing that has to do with my job makes sense to you," she remarked bitterly. "Anyway, I've been asked to make a speech to this group, so how can you say women are totally excluded?"

"Because we both know it's true." He paused. "Are they going to allow you to eat at the head table and stay for the whole affair?"

"No, because I'm not a member."

"Oh. And we know that you couldn't become a member if you wanted to be. Because you're a woman."

Suzanna didn't respond, and there were a few minutes of uncomfortable silence. Then she started to laugh. "You will appreciate this—my mother wants to crash their party."

"Your mother? Bully for her! Why?"

"She wants me to let her in to speak to Mr. O'Hara." Suzanna shook her head. "Want to know the worst part? I agreed. But who can refuse their mother? I've been worried about it all week."

"I'm sure she can take care of herself."

"I'm not worried about her! It's me! Rutherford would be furious if he knew I'd plotted to invade his precious private party."

"This doesn't really sound like Ellie. Why does she want to do it?"

"My energetic mother has a fabulous new project. She's found something that is interesting and time-consuming. For her, though, it's been *all*-consuming."

"Isn't that what you wanted?"

"Yes. I wanted her to be busy and happy. But I must admit that 'all-consuming' was not in my plan."

"What's she doing?"

"Recording Wordsworth for the county library."

He laughed. "What is Wordsworth?"

"She's taping oral histories from many of the elderly members of our community for a permanent record in the county library. It's really very innovative, and I'm proud of her."

"Then what's the problem?"

"She's so zealous. That's all she talks about, and now—" Suzanna gestured "—she has this idea, and when she asked for my help, I didn't have the heart to tell her no."

"How does this connect with her invading the Rogues' meeting?"

"Oh, she doesn't want to cause trouble. She just wants in. You see, she's been trying to reach Mr. O'Hara to discuss his contribution to Wordsworth. Her committee has encouraged her to get an in-depth, detailed history of how his father and uncle started the department store."

"Sounds interesting."

"I agree. But Mother can't get to him. His secretary keeps giving her the runaround. Says he's out or that she'll give him the message. But he never calls back. And once he canceled an appointment and didn't tell her. She got all dressed and went down to his office. Oh, Chase, she was so disappointed."

"I can understand that."

"So Mama wants to confront him, face-to-face, in a place where he can't easily escape. She plans on telling him how valuable his family's history is to this county. She thinks if she talks directly to him, he won't refuse."

Chase grinned. "She's probably right. What a spunky lady she is."

"I'll say. She's changing so much, I never know what to expect every time I see her. She changed her hairstyle, had it cut real short. Do you know that she actually brought fast-food fried chicken to my house the other night?"

"I do it all the time. Is that revolutionary?"

"For Mama, it is." Suzanna laughed. "She tried to pass it off as her own!"

"Let her alone, Suzanna. Let her change."

"I'm trying." She shook her head. "But what she wants to do with the Rogues Club could backfire."

"And what's the worst thing that could happen? She could get kicked out? Or, in her case, they would politely ask her to leave. So, what's wrong with that?"

"Worst-case scenario is that my job could be in jeopardy over it." She looked away. "I know you don't consider that a tragedy."

"You're right." He grabbed her and turned her to face toward him. "But I wouldn't want anything to happen to jeopardize your staying here, Suzanna."

"Well, losing my job certainly would."

"I don't . . ." He moved closer. "Don't want . . ." He rubbed her nose with his. "To lose you. . . ." He kissed her gently on the lips, then kissed her again with more fervor. They were as close as too bulky coats would let them be, but it wasn't close enough for Chase. He pulled her up with him. "What we have, Suzanna, is too good to lose."

"I feel the same way, Chase."

He wrapped his arms around her shoulders and hugged her. "You cold?"

"A little."

"I'd like to warm you." He lowered his head and kissed her again. His lips were warm and inviting. He wanted to hold her inside his coat, wanted to press her to him. "Come with me for a little ride."

"On the cycle?" She gave him a wary glance. "I'm not twice a fool."

"I'll be careful. No wrecks, I promise." His mahogany eyes gleamed. "I want to show you something."

"It looks like rain."

"This won't take long."

Being with him had given her some of her best moments. She wasn't really afraid of riding with him. She knew that the wreck had been an unavoidable accident. It wouldn't—couldn't—happen again. He obviously wanted to share something with her. And, she wanted to go with him. Besides, no one would know.

"Okay."

He clutched her hand. "Come on!" Together they raced to the bike and mounted it.

She clutched his waist.

"Stay close, Suz. Go with me."

She shifted and brought her thighs alongside his. Even beneath his corduroy jeans and leather jacket, she could feel the ripple of muscles. *Go with me.* Once again, she was more than ready to go with him.

So, what was wrong with that? Chase was her kind of man. The machine revved to life beneath them, and

Suzanna clutched Chase tightly around the waist, closed her eyes, and let herself fly off into the wild blue with him.

8

AS THEY WHIRLED AWAY in the cool, late afternoon, Suzanna didn't feel cold at all. His body shielded her. She ducked her head and pressed against his strong back, loving every second with him.

When they stopped near a thicket of pines, she was almost sorry to see the ride end so soon. He helped her off the cycle and took her hand. As Suzanna slid her palm against his, she felt again the pull of their mutual attraction. They walked toward the river.

She could see anticipation build in Chase as they drew closer. It made her happy to think that he wanted to share something special with her. With every step, her curiosity grew stronger.

"What is it, Chase? What could possibly be way out here?"

"You'll see." He smiled at her mysteriously.

He led her directly to the edge of a little bluff overlooking the river and pointed down to a square houseboat that bobbed against a crude wooden pier. "Just bought it yesterday," he said proudly.

"For the float-fishing tours?"

He nodded. "The first of about three or four boats I plan to buy."

"Chase! How wonderful!" She smiled broadly. "I'm so glad you went after it."

"With no help from anyone," he muttered. His bitterness spilled over whenever he thought about how tough it was for him to make it in this town.

She squeezed his hand. "What's it like inside? It looks big."

"Big enough. Want to see it?"

She looked over the edge. "Can we get down there?"

"Over this way." He indicated a path that angled down to the river.

"Why is it docked way out here? Are you hiding it?"

"I just don't want everyone to have a chance to speculate on what I'm doing. I don't want the public to get wind of my plans until I'm ready for them to know. I expect to have several of these ready to go by spring, when the announcement is made." He helped her climb down the steep terrain. "That way, we'll coincide publicity with availability."

"That's a smart business move."

"This vessel is sound but needs a lot of work." He pointed out chipped paint as they drew closer. "And the bottom needs scraping. Another reason for having it in this cove is that we can pull it up on the bank and do the work right here. Want to go aboard?"

"Sure."

He tugged on the tie rope until the boat was close enough to step over to and helped her on. The sway of the craft was minimal because of its wide, flat bottom. "This will be the best equipped and largest boat in the fleet. The rest of them will be much smaller, flat johnboats. This one isn't designed for long-term excursions, but a large party could rent it for all day. And a small group could take it overnight."

Suzanna followed Chase around the outer porch, listening as he talked about the changes he intended to make. The boat bounced a little more as the wind began to whip up a frenzy. Small white caps appeared on the normally calm river, and the waves created soft, suctionlike noises under the boat. The water turned from clear to an ominous opaque.

"And in here—" Chase ducked his head and entered the door to the interior "—the beds are small and the kitchen barely adequate, but the bathroom, she works. Not quite the comforts of home, but close."

Suzanna straightened her mussed hair as she took in the four cot-size beds, the kitchen sink and tiny refrigerator, and the small door that led to a minute bathroom. "It isn't very roomy, but in my opinion, it beats an open boat. At least it has a toilet."

He leaned against the short counter next to the sink. "Yep, I'd say that's a prerequisite for any long-term trip."

"Actually, Chase, it's kind of nice and cozy in here."

"Not much privacy for large parties."

"How many does it accommodate?"

"Designed for up to about fifteen." He paused. "Or as few as two."

She ran her hand along one of the beds. "It would be nice to take a float trip on the White River in a boat like this."

"With the right person, it could be . . . perfect."

"You could promote it as the perfect fishing trip."

"Yes, uh, right. Perfect fishing."

The nearness of Chase disturbed her, but Suzanna tried to ignore it. She examined the cabin and pretended to concentrate on her surroundings rather than his strong hands and the bulge in his jeans as he leaned against the counter. She kept moving, though fully aware of him.

A scattering noise on the roof startled her, and she looked up. "What—"

"Rain," he announced in a low voice. "We just made it."

"Rain? I told you!" She ran to the door. Heavy drops peppered the deck and a gray mist surrounded the boat. "We're caught!"

His tone was quiet and calm compared to hers. "I prefer to think we're sheltered. At least we aren't getting wet."

"But what about Ross?" she wailed. "I left him fishing. He'll get soaked!"

"Don't worry, Suzanna." Chase moved to stand close behind her at the door. "Bo'll take care of him. Until we get back."

"Bo?" She whirled around. Chase's arms braced the small doorframe on either side of her. He was so near that she could see the tiny lines that fanned from the corners of his deep brown eyes. Her mouth felt dry, and she struggled in an effort to remain coherent. "Bo's there?"

"Bo's always there. And he knows to take care of Ken, and Ross, if I'm not around. He'll watch after them until we get back, Suz-anna." He drawled her name in a low whisper. "So we can relax until this stops."

"Getting caught in the rain with me is starting to be a habit, isn't it, Chase? I think you planned this."

"I have no power over the rain, or anything else around here. But being alone with you is a habit I like."

He bent forward and kissed her lips. "You like it, too, from the way you react. You just don't want to show it."

She remembered what Mr. Rutherford had said about habits developing more habits. And she realized that she, too, was developing a habit with Chase. "We . . . we really shouldn't—"

He took both her hands, lacing their fingers, pressing their palms together. "Shouldn't what? Be alone? Can't be helped."

Her eyes met his in a smoky gaze. "Shouldn't let anything happen."

"Like what?"

"Like what happened last time."

"You mean the night you came to my place? You aren't blaming me for that, are you?"

"No," she said in a low, guilty voice. "Like . . . what you're thinking might happen again."

"Can you read my mind, too? My, my, Suzanna, you're talented."

"Doesn't take a genius to recognize that look in your eyes, Chase Clements." The passion he generated between them unnerved her.

"I see that same look in your eyes, too." He shifted and brought his shoulders closer. They almost filled the doorway.

She could feel her reserve faltering.

"Why not give way? Why can't you let your feelings out and admit to this wonderful thing we share?"

"It isn't good . . . for either of us." She looked into his eyes—dark, sensual, inviting.

"Says who? Feels good to me." His face lowered slowly to hers.

She couldn't move. "Chase—"

His lips met hers with demanding force. The kiss seared her lips and took her breath away. What little resistance she had left in her vanished as she softened against him. His hands moved to her hips. She arched her back and thrust her breasts outward, wanting to shed her thick coat and feel him next to her.

"There, now," he whispered, his lips nibbling at hers. "Wasn't that good?"

"Yes. Chase, you know I can't resist you."

"Good. 'Cause I can't resist you, either, Suz." He began unbuttoning her coat. "I just wanted you to see that this is good for both of us. That you're responding to me."

"Who wouldn't, Chase?" She felt weak-kneed as his hands opened her coat and reached inside.

His hands stroked her breasts, moved down her sides and around to embrace her bottom. "No red-blooded male that I know." He pressed her to his erection. "Come on. Celebrate the fact that you're a woman—" one hand slid between her legs "—and I'm a man."

"I know, Chase . . ."

"I want you, Suzanna." His hands touched her everywhere through her clothes. "Don't you want me?"

"Yes, Chase. You know I do." She had to have him.

Chase had removed his coat and hovered over her a moment as she lay back on one of the cot-size beds. He lay down beside her. His lips captured hers. As passion overcame him, his kiss became more demanding and he forced her lips open to receive his tongue.

Suzanna's searching hands went under his sweater and stroked the muscled length of his back. She felt his body respond with a jolt when she placed her hands behind, beneath his waistband, and cupped each tight buttock.

Instinctively he thrust forward. He found her receptive and willing. Both of them were eager. He covered her breasts with kisses as he unfastened her slacks.

Urgently she clutched at the opening of his jeans. He groaned when she reached inside and gently squeezed his crotch.

Somehow their clothes were discarded. Feverishly he dug into his billfold for protection.

"Prepared, Chase?"

"Always prepared when I'm with you, Suzanna."

"You always have the right answers." She wanted to believe that he slept only with her. Right now, though, all she desperately wanted was for him to love her. With a welcoming smile, she opened her arms to him.

They came together in urgent frenzy. His hair-roughened chest crushed the tender velvet of her breasts. She squirmed with pleasure as he wedged between her knees, then pressed open her thighs.

His kisses were hot and hard. His pulsing heat aggressively sought her. She arched, trembling and calling his name.

She clutched his back, digging her fingers into his shoulders, pulling him more tightly to her. He responded to her eagerness by thrusting himself fully into her.

"Easy, Suz," he murmured. "Slow down." With deliberate patience, he paused, holding off the exquisite crescendo for as long as possible.

"I can't." She rocked slowly, concentrating on the buildup of sensations created by their friction, savoring his maleness. "Can't stop—can't wait," she gasped.

With a little cry, Suzanna started to move vigorously against him.

Chase picked up her rhythm and drove her over the edge. The fervency of her spasms pulled him with her into ecstasy.

Eventually, reality intruded and they remembered that they lay in the cold, damp interior of a secluded houseboat. Still they clung together, reluctant to let go, to lose each other, to accept the inevitable.

He kissed her cheek, then her earlobe. "Ahh, Suz, this is no way for us to celebrate what we share—slipping around at night and meeting in cold, damp places."

She sighed. "I know."

"I want you at home, by my fire."

"You have to admit, there's a certain excitement in meeting like this." She smiled and ran her hands over his buttocks.

They slid apart.

She combed her fingertips through the curly mat on his chest. "It was very good, Chase. Very."

"The best," he murmured and kissed her again. "Suzanna, I don't want to lose you...don't want to lose what we have."

"What *do* we have, Chase? A friendship? A casual affair?"

"Both." He stroked her silky jet hair. "Only I'd call this a hot affair." He nuzzled her neck. "Whatever it is, it's special. I think of holding you like this all the time."

"What do you want, Chase?"

"You."

"You have me. Now, what?"

He sighed and pulled her closer. "I want to make passionate love to you all night, any night or every night. And I especially want to wake up the next morning with you still beside me in my bed. I'm tired of sneaking around like this."

She tried to laugh. "I thought that's what you liked so much about this relationship—the clandestine meetings."

He kissed her nose. "You are what I like so much about this relationship, Suzanna. *You.* So, what are you going to do about it, Suz?"

"I . . . I don't know, Chase."

"Be honest with yourself. Then you'll know."

"I'm trying."

"What do you want, Suz? What do you want out of this?"

She turned her face away, but he pressed it back so that she had to look at him. She couldn't avoid looking directly into his beautiful eyes. "You, Chase. I want you."

"You have me," he returned. "But only secretly."

She was quiet for a minute. "I want more, Chase. But I'm afraid what we're doing here is no good for either of us."

"Then we'll come out of hiding."

"No!" Her eyes widened. The thought of discovery terrified her even more. "That won't help. We both have other responsibilities besides ourselves."

"You mean, then people would know you've been fooling around with me. And your precious reputation would be damaged."

"Chase, that's ridiculous."

His mouth hardened. "It's because I'm the bad apple and you're trying to be so damned good!"

He heaved himself off her and began pulling on his clothes. She ran to him and clutched his hands. "No! No, Chase!" Her eyes revealed the truth of his words, and she turned away guiltily.

In that uncomfortable moment, when they both angrily faced each other with their clothes half off, she knew. *She knew!* What she was denying to herself, to him, and most of all, to everyone else, was that she had fallen helplessly in love with him. But he couldn't possibly know what that meant. And she wasn't sure that she did, either.

"Then what?" His voice was loud and rough, like an exploding cannon. "What is it, Suzanna?"

"What I need—" her voice was low and trembling "—you can't give me."

"What is it? What the hell are you talking about? Sex? I thought that was pretty good."

"It is . . . was. Extremely good."

"What is it, then, Suzanna?" He whirled her around in his arms. "What is it? Anything! I'll give you anything: Love? I'll give you more love than you can handle! Money? A car? Something for Ross?"

She stared at him and swallowed hard. She wasn't even sure of herself, sure of what she meant. But she knew she'd never had what she needed from Zack. And she couldn't make that mistake again. "Of course not. Don't be insulting."

He shoved her away. "I think you just want an excuse to end this!"

"Maybe." She sat down on the narrow bed where they'd made love, her hands clenched in her lap. "Maybe I don't really know what I want, Chase."

He jerked his clothes on, then stood angrily, watching her. "Tell you what, Suzanna. When you decide what it is that you want, let me know."

His tone was angry. But his expression was hurt. When she dressed, she went to him. "Chase, it has nothing to do with our...affair, if that's what you want to call it, or with what we mean as friends to each other. It's my problem. And it has to do with the past."

"Don't bring up the past with me, Suzanna. You know how I feel about it."

She put her hand on his cheek. Then, with both hands framing his face, she pulled him down for a kiss. "Don't abandon me, Chase. I need you."

Chase wrapped his arms around her and held her close for a long, long time. He raised his head. "Listen."

"I don't hear anything."

"It's stopped raining. We'd better be going while we can."

"Yes." Reluctantly Suzanna left with Chase, knowing there was no avoiding the real world of jobs and families and responsibilities.

On the motorcycle they doubled back to where her Toyota was parked. Then they parted and Chase led the way while she followed him to Bo's small apartment. He motioned for her to wait and, in a few minutes, returned with Ken and Ross.

"Hey, Mom!" Ross exclaimed, clambering into the passenger seat. "We didn't catch any fish. So Bo fixed hot dogs. He makes great home fries!"

"You've already eaten?"

"We were hungry." He shrugged.

"Growing boys gotta eat," Chase said, making a teasing grab at Ken who stood nearby.

"But it seems that Bo's doing more than his share of feeding my son these days," Suzanna remarked, looking pointedly at Chase.

"It's okay," Ken said. "Bo's used to feeding me all the time."

Chase grinned at the boy. "That's because you're always hungry." He looked back at Suzanna. "I supplement Bo's grocery supplies, though, so don't worry about it."

"Well, I'll see what I can do to repay him in some way, too," she said. Then she looked at Ken. "We're going to rent a movie for the VCR Friday night, Ken. Would you like to come over and watch it with Ross?"

"A movie? Hey, yeah! That'd be great! You have a VCR?"

She nodded. It was one of the few things Zack ever bought for them. "Plan to have supper, too. Probably pizza."

Ken turned to Chase. "Can I go, Dad?"

"Sure."

The two boys cheered rowdily. "I'll rent something good!" Ross promised.

Suzanna put the car into reverse, but before she released the brake, she said, "And bring your dad, too. If he doesn't already have plans."

Ken grinned and looked up at Chase for an answer. Suzanna looked at him, too.

"I'll be there," he answered quietly. "If you're sure."

"I'm sure."

"Good luck on Thursday's luncheon."

"Thanks." She waved and drove off.

As usual, Ross chatted happily about his experiences at the Boon Docks. "And when it turned cold and started to rain, Bo invited us in for hot chocolate and a bite to eat. I figured you wouldn't mind. He's a real good cook, Mom. I was a little worried about you, but he said you probably got caught in the rain. Is that what happened?"

Suzanna gripped the steering wheel and guiltily thought about what had really happened while she was gone. Was it wrong to lie to herself about Chase and keep meeting him like this? How could she admit to anyone that she was crazy about him? But, how could she do without him?

"Mom?"

"Yes, Ross, that's what happened."

"Mom, thanks for inviting Ken over Friday night. We're going to have lots of fun! Wonder what kind of movies he likes. Can we get *Friday the 13th?*"

"Absolutely not! Maybe something with humor." She gave him a scolding glance. "I expect you to clean your room before Friday."

"Yes, ma'am." He was quiet a minute. "Are you and Chase going to watch the movies with us?"

"I don't know."

"You'll probably sit in the kitchen and talk, like grown-ups usually do." He made a face. "Bor-ing."

"Probably."

CHASE WATCHED the red taillights of Suzanna's Toyota disappear over the hill. He drove Ken back to their little home and proceeded to lay a fire in the hearth. He was so quiet over the next few hours that before he went to bed, Ken approached Chase. "Dad, are you mad about something?"

"No, son."

"Are you sick?"

"No, why do you ask?"

"You're acting so strange tonight, I thought maybe I'd done something wrong."

"Believe me, I'd let you know." Chase poked at the fire. "Just have a lot on my mind, son, that's all. You know how adults worry about things."

"Oh." Ken shuffled. "Brother! It's a real drag being an adult, huh?"

"Isn't it your bedtime?"

"That's what you always say when you want me to leave you alone." Ken shuffled away. "G'night, Dad."

"G'night." Chase thought about their exchange for a few minutes, then went into Ken's dark room. He left the door open and let the light shine onto the floor. "I don't want you to worry about my problems, Ken. I'll work them out. Anyway, they don't concern you, okay?"

"Yeah. It's not about my mother?"

"No, son."

"I'll bet it's about Suzanna, then."

He bent down and kissed the boy's forehead. "I love you, Ken. I won't let anything happen to you."

"I love you, too, Dad."

God, how he loved that kid! He didn't know what he'd do if Darlene ever showed up again. And yet, he knew she would. Someday.

He just hoped his relationship with Ken was strong enough to survive any obstacles. He wouldn't worry about that now. Hell, he had enough to handle, trying to sort out his relationship with Suzanna. He went into the kitchen and poured himself a double shot of Jack Daniel's whiskey.

The way he felt about Suzanna was different from what he'd ever felt for any woman. Oh, he was physically attracted to her. That much was the same, but who wouldn't be?

But there was something else about Suzanna for him. When they were together, he felt so comfortable, so through-and-through *good*, that he wanted to be with her all the time. He took a sip of the bourbon.

They did make good lovers! No woman could ever compare. Chase took a deep breath and let it out slowly. No, that wasn't it. It was more. He also wanted to help her, to listen to her, to make her happy.

This was getting treacherous! He lifted his glass up and took a big gulp. It burned his throat, and he hoped it would dull the slow burn deep inside for Suzanna. Unfortunately, he knew that nothing short of having her in his life would do that.

9

AT DAWN ON THURSDAY, Suzanna's feet hit the floor running and didn't slow to a walk all day. She didn't really mind being so busy. What she did mind was the everything-at-the-last-minute effort to pull off the Rogues Club luncheon.

Besides a double column list of To Do's clamped to her clipboard, she also worried about the fact that her formerly docile mother was definitely going to slip into the all-male domain and confront Mr. O'Hara. And Suzanna had to hide that fact from her boss. She felt like the cat that walked the fence separating two vicious bulldogs and at the halfway mark, got her tail caught in a crack in the boards.

"Suzanna?"

She looked up from her speech notes to see the very person she did *not* want to encounter today: Alec McNeil.

"Hope I'm not interrupting anything." He smiled and stepped into her office. "I wanted to know if you received the correct meat delivery yesterday."

"Yes, Alec. Thank you. Everything was exactly right."

"Good." With an expectant smile on his lean face, he moved farther into the room. "And what about the delivery? Was it on time? Was the deliveryman polite?"

"No complaints."

He took a seat in the Victorian chair next to her desk. "What about quality? Have you checked out those chickens?"

"Not personally." Alec was so sincere that Suzanna swallowed a quip about chickens being the least of her worries. Instead, she answered with a polite but businesslike "The chef seems pleased."

"Good, good." He nodded several times as he repeated the word.

Suzanna could see that he was struggling to make conversation with her, but she could only think of the million-and-two things she had to do or make sure were done in the next hour.

Finally he summoned his courage. "I've been trying to reach you, Suzanna."

"I know, Alec. I got your messages, and I apologize for not returning your calls. I've been extremely busy the last couple of weeks. This luncheon has kept me hopping."

"I see."

"No, you don't," she replied, trying to be diplomatic. "This place wasn't ready for a luncheon, but Mr. Rutherford insisted that we make the effort for the prestigious Rogues Club. And the total responsibility fell into my lap since I'm the manager. Now, I'd like to sit and chat, Alec, but I just can't do it today. I hope you understand."

"Yeah. Sure." He looked down at his hands, which were clasped nervously between his knees. With renewed purpose, he looked up at her. "I just wondered if we could go out again, Suzanna. I really enjoyed the evening we spent together and hope you did, too."

"Yes, it was lovely." Lying was not Suzanna's style and she wondered why she was doing it. In the back of her mind, she was remembering what she'd done with Chase *after* the date with Alec.

"Well, Suzanna, what about this weekend?"

A weaker person would have agreed to go with him again. Alec was, after all, a very nice guy. And she probably *should* give him another chance.

No. She'd been weak once. But that was before Chase. Now, *any* other man paled in comparison, and she had no inclination to try to fool herself anymore. Or pretend to the poor man who sat before her.

Today, she was strong. She was a businesswoman in charge. For further reinforcement, she had worn her "power clothes"—the gray pin-striped suit and purple silk blouse. She felt invincible. So, she had to be fair— with herself as well as Alec.

"I'm sorry, but I'm busy this weekend, Alec," she said. *Coward!* she thought. *Be honest. Tell him.*

"Okay." He stood and looked at her hopefully. "Maybe another time."

"Maybe." She stood also, in time to catch a flurry of movement behind Alec. Its source was her mother, who was waving for attention from the hall outside her office!

"Look, Suzanna," Alec began, "I know one date is too soon to tell, but I'd like to know where I stand with you. Whether we have a chance."

She looked up at him. He was asking for honesty. So why was she hesitating? It wasn't like her to pussyfoot around, and that's all she'd been doing since she returned to Grace. With Alec. With Mr. Rutherford. Even with her own mother. It was all part of what she thought she *should* do. And it just wasn't working.

"Actually, Alec, I like you very much." Suzanna paused to smile encouragingly. "But honestly, there aren't any sparks between us. You know?" She felt a little frazzled as her mother waved again from the doorway.

"You don't think those sparks could develop if we gave them another chance?"

At the moment, Suzanna felt like shouting "No! Never!" and shoving Alec out the door. And jerking her sweet-faced mother inside—and hiding her. Instead, she had to stand there having a delicate conversation with Alec. "I think . . . not," she answered. "I'm sorry if you think I led you on, Alec. I like you. A lot. I hope we can be friends."

"I'm disappointed. But I can't say you led me on, Suzanna. And at least you're honest."

She smiled with relief. Maybe she'd managed to save their friendship *and* his dignity. "I, uh, someone needs to see me about something, so I'd better go, Alec."

"Sure. I won't keep you any longer. I'll look forward to your speech, Suzanna."

"Oh? That's right. You're a member of the Rogues."

"Seems like almost everybody in this town is a member."

Not the women, she thought as she walked to the door with him. *And not Chase.* "My concern right now is feeding them."

"You'll do a fine job, I'm sure." He couldn't hide his disappointment. "See you later, Suzanna."

Ellie turned her back on Alec and discreetly ducked her head as he left the office. Then she dashed inside and closed the door.

Suzanna smiled at how impressive her innovative mother looked today in her navy-and-white suit and perky little hat nestled in her gray curls. Ellie, too, had worn her "power clothes." "Is that a new outfit, Mama?"

"Do you like it?" Ellie asked, suddenly revealing her apprehension. She held her arms out and spun around. "What do you think? Is it too much?"

Suzanna broke into laughter and clapped her hands together. "I love it!"

Ellie smoothed her skirt. "Are you sure?"

"It's perfect!" Suzanna gave her a quick hug and adjusted the large navy bow at the juncture of the white collar. "Navy and white are your colors. Mr. O'Hara won't be able to turn away from you today."

"Are you sure this is going to be okay, Suzanna?"

"It's going to be just fine, Mama. Now, don't you worry about me. You take care of your business today."

"What about if your boss—"

Suzanna held up one hand to halt her mother. "He won't have a thing to say about this. Anyway, it's possible that you can speak to Mr. O'Hara and be gone without Mr. Rutherford even knowing about it." Doubtful, she thought. But possible.

"Hallie and Ann helped me shop for this suit." Ellie brushed lightly at her bosom. "And Mary Ellen loaned me this cute little hat to match."

"What gives, Mama? You mean half the town knows what you're doing?"

"Not the town. Just the ladies. They're all behind me, one hundred percent."

Suzanna pretended to slap her forehead. "And I've been trying to keep this a secret!"

"They won't tell a soul."

"Are you kidding?" Suzanna scoffed. "Most of those women's husbands belong to the Rogues! Do you really expect them to keep quiet?"

"I certainly do." Ellie straightened her shoulders. "In fact, young lady, several of them admitted that they envied me. And said if I didn't follow through with this, they would. They don't appreciate the way Mr. O'Hara has treated me."

"Neither do I, Mama. That's why I'm all for what you're doing today."

"I do appreciate it, Suzanna. But if this doesn't work, we have another tactic up our sleeves."

"What?"

"Well, it's still in the talking stage, but we women might consider boycotting O'Hara's business. Then he'd listen."

"He sure would." Suzanna shook her head and grinned. "What's this town coming to?"

"We are coming into our own. We're using our heads and deciding that we can make decisions and have power in this town. That's what we're coming to."

Ellie's proud announcement made Suzanna take notice. This was no small matter. It had widespread ramifications that would ripple through the entire female population of Grace. "I think you're right, Mama. And it's about time."

"It's the principle, sugar." Ellie's blue eyes sparkled. "Those men think they're so high-'n'-mighty that they can have their elite little club and keep women out, but we'll show them, won't we?"

We? Suzanna sighed, wondering what kind of sacrifice this would take on her part. "We sure will, Mama."

Ellie smiled sweetly. "I have a mission. And I won't stop until I reach Mr. O'Hara."

"Well, today's your day. He'll be here soon." Suzanna checked her watch. "In fact, everyone will be. I'd better be going, Mama. I'm having a preluncheon meeting with the waiters."

Ellie placed her hand on Suzanna's arm. "I couldn't help noticing you and Alec in here talking so seriously. Are you two . . . ?"

"No, Mama." Time for some honesty, she decided.

"No?" Ellie looked puzzled. "No, what?"

"No, nothing, Mama. We aren't doing anything."

"Oh." Ellie's expression turned to disappointment. "Well, you don't have to tell me about your private affairs."

Suzanna wondered what her mother would think of her "private affair" with Chase Clements. "I don't mind telling you that Alec and I aren't seeing each other. We aren't an item. We don't click. No sparks."

Ellie looked hurt. "I'm sorry, Suzanna."

"Well, I'm not." Suzanna smiled. "It's okay, Mama. I'd better hurry to make that meeting." She paused at the door. "Good luck, Mama."

Ellie gave her daughter a brave smile. "Thank you, Suzanna. You've given me the courage."

Suzanna left her mother, hoping that she'd given Ellie "courage."

BY THE TIME SUZANNA had finished her speech to the Rogues, she was a nervous wreck. Not that the speech didn't go smoothly; with notes in front of her, she'd been completely in charge. But out of the corner of her eye, she could see her mother standing in a side doorway, listening and waiting for her opportunity with Mr. O'Hara.

At the end, Suzanna accepted the polite applause, handed out her rush-printed membership forms and took her leave of the male-dominated hall. Then she waited in her office, trying to make herself busy, trying to forget that her own dear mother was doing her thing upstairs.

Suzanna said a little prayer that Ellie would be successful in her "mission." And she hoped that her own job wouldn't be placed at risk by her mother's actions. By now, everyone, including Old Man Rutherford, must know that Suzanna was one of Ellie's strongest supporters. She couldn't help but smile at the thought of all those sweet little ladies in town, probably waiting at Ellie's house right now, to see if she'd made it.

When her office door burst open and Mr. Rutherford blustered in without so much as a polite knock, Suzanna wasn't terribly surprised. She gazed at him expectantly. She had, in fact, been the cat walking the fence, and now her tail was caught in a crack.

"Suzanna—"

"Yes?" She rested one hand casually on her desktop. She hid the other—a white-knuckled fist—in her lap.

He turned back toward the open. "Please come on in, Mrs. Schafer," he said in a mockingly sweet voice. Then he glared at Suzanna.

She looked back at him, amazed at her own steadiness.

Ellie entered the office with a wry smile on her sweet face. Her gaze met Suzanna's triumphantly and out of Rutherford's view her hand formed a discreet "okay" sign. She'd done it! Mission accomplished!

Suzanna smiled instantly. "Mama! How nice to see you here."

Rutherford's voice boomed in the tiny office. "Do you know what she's been up to?"

"I'm afraid so."

"And you let her?"

"Let her? I *encouraged* her. After all, Mr. Rutherford, she *is* my mother. And I don't want anyone treating her rudely. Even someone as bigshot as Mr. O'Hara. As you'd probably agree, she can take care of herself, if given the opportunity." And the push, she added mentally.

While he blustered, Ellie stepped forward and confronted him. "Now, Don, Suzanna isn't to blame for any of this. Let me explain how it all happened...."

Suzanna stood back and let Ellie take charge of the situation. It was obvious that this was as important to her as facing O'Hara. And no matter what happened, she was so proud of her mother that she could shout.

Suzanna had looked forward to Friday night with a passion. She'd even bought two different pizzas— hamburger and pepperoni for the boys, and mushroom and black olive for her and Chase. Ken's face lit up when he saw the pizza, soft drinks and popcorn already laid out on the coffee table in the living room.

Beanbag chairs and throw pillows were also in place. "Thanks, Mrs. Schafer. This is great!"

"Ken, why don't you start calling me Suzanna?" She placed her hand on his shoulder. "My mother is Mrs. Schafer." Ross had been calling Chase by his first name for some time, and she wanted the same kind of friendly relationship with Ken.

The boy gave Chase a quick, questioning glance. Receiving an approving nod, he shyly complied. "Okay, uh, Suzanna."

Chase smiled at her. "Good idea. After all, we're friends. Right, guys?"

"All right!" Ross gave Chase a high five, then turned to Ken. "You ready to eat? I'm starved!"

"Yeah! What movie did you get? Hey, this is my favorite kind of pizza. How did you know, Mrs. Sch— er, Suzanna?"

"I let Ross order it."

The boys scrambled noisily for pizza slices, switched on the VCR and began to get settled.

As Ross had predicted, Suzanna and Chase slipped into the kitchen to talk. Immediately, Chase closed the louvered door between the two rooms and took her in his arms.

She glowed in the warmth of his embrace. "Chase—"

"Don't say a word." His kiss was strong and passionate. And wonderfully long. When he finally raised his head, he sighed. "I've missed that. Missed *you*, pretty lady."

"Me, too, Chase. Missed you. It's been a long week without you."

"But you made it, obviously. With your job intact?"

"Oh, yes. You'd have heard about it if I'd gotten fired."

"I hope so. That's what friends are for. And this is what lovers are for." He kissed her again.

His tongue teased her lips open, tracing the sensitive insides, then darted in and out. She dipped her tongue into the minty-tasting recesses of his mouth. His hands moved down her back, stroking her hips as if he couldn't get enough of her.

Lifting her arms to circle his shoulders, she molded her full length to him. Every part of her responded to the feel of him. Her body writhed in sensual pleasure, and the familiar currents of desire began to ripple through her.

Spreading his legs, he grasped her thighs with his, thus halting her erotic movements. "Hold it," he murmured. "Unless you're ready to follow through."

"Chase, you do certain things to me. I can't help it."

"We could slip out the back door and finish this." His lips teased her neck.

"Baby, it's cold outside, in case you've forgotten."

"We could crawl in the truck."

"'Crawl' is right. No, thanks. I outgrew that fifteen years ago."

"How about the kitchen table, then?"

"Chase!" she scolded in a whisper. "We have children in the next room."

"We'll be quiet." He caught her earlobe between his teeth.

"I have a better idea."

"Slip down to my house for a few minutes?"

"This one is longer lasting."

"I like the sound of it already."

"But you have to wait."

"I've spent my life waiting for you, my love. Now I'd like to make up for lost time."

"Will next week be soon enough?"

"All week?"

"Three days."

"Three days? And nights?"

"Yep. Out of town."

"You mean I'll get to wake up in the morning with you by my side?"

"I promise."

"You got it. I'm game. That may be worth the wait, after all. How are you going to arrange this?"

"Mr. Rutherford is arranging it."

"My kind of guy. And all this time I thought he was my enemy."

"He doesn't know he's doing us a favor."

"Even better." His thumbs roamed her breasts, caressing the firm tips. "Now, are you going to tell me what you're talking about, or do we launch into twenty questions?"

"Mr. Rutherford has agreed to send me to a two-day seminar on resort management in Little Rock next week. And you're invited—privately, of course."

"Rutherford's footing the bill? What a generous man!"

"Old Man Rutherford doesn't know. And if you breathe a word of this, I'm a dead duck. But I figured if we were discreet—and we've been pretty discreet so far—we can pull it off."

"I don't know if I can wait a whole week for you, but I'll try. When?"

"Wednesday and Thursday."

"I happen to be free. But for you, Suz, I'd be free anytime."

Just as he lowered his head for another kiss, Ross yelled from the living room, "Hey, Mom! Gramma's here! Her car just pulled up!"

Suzanna froze in Chase's arms. "Mama?" Her mind spun around searching for possible ideas for keeping her mother away. They had a close-knit, casual relationship that often included unannounced visits. So how could she explain Ken and the truck parked out front without revealing Chase? She pushed away from him.

"Shall I slip out the back door?"

"You? No! Don't be ridiculous!" Suzanna laughed nervously. "Anyway, she's already seen your truck. No. I'll go meet her. You...stay put." She motioned toward the oven and refrigerator. "There's pizza, diet pop..." She closed the louvered doors behind her and dashed to the front door before Ellie could get there—and possibly walk right in.

Suzanna opened the door with a brave smile. "Hi, Mama. Come on in."

Chase could hear Suzanna greeting Ellie at the door. She'd probably visit for a few minutes, then politely wait for Ellie to leave. He poured a glass of diet cola and listened at the louvered door.

"Mama, I want you to meet Ross's *best* friend, Ken Clements. He came over to watch a movie with Ross." She put her arm around Ellie's shoulders. "Ken, this is my mother, Mrs. Schafer."

"My pleasure, Mrs. Schafer."

Suzanna was impressed when Ken stood and shook hands with the older woman. Chase had taught the boy manners, too.

"It's nice to meet you, Ken." Ellie smiled at the boy, then looked curiously at Suzanna.

"Gramma!" Ross motioned to the half-finished pizza on the table. "Have some pizza with us. Want to watch the movie?"

"Well, thanks, sugar—"

"You two go ahead and watch your movie, Ross." Suzanna put her arm around her mother's shoulders and steered her toward the kitchen. "We'll have our pizza in here."

The game was over. She was ready for some openness. Whatever made her think she could keep Chase a secret forever, anyway? No matter what happened, she had to let her mother know that she and Chase were friends. And maybe sometime in the future, she'd reveal that they were more than friends. It was time to be blunt with her own mother. She pushed the door open.

Chase was pouring a third diet cola over ice. The table was set for three, with the steaming pizza in the center. He looked up, as if expecting Ellie to join them. "Hi. Ready for pizza?" he asked with his appealingly crooked smile.

"Mama, I want you to meet *my good friend*, Chase Clements."

Ellie gaped at the ruggedly handsome man standing in Suzanna's kitchen. It didn't take a genius to figure what was happening here. Drawing on her Southern breeding and charm, she smiled politely. "It's nice to meet you, Mr. Clements."

"My pleasure entirely, Mrs. Schafer." Chase extended his hand. "I've been wanting to meet you for a long time."

The fixed smile remained on Ellie's face and her eyebrows rose slightly.

"We were just about to have some pizza, Mama. Please join us." Suzanna gently manipulated her mother into the chair Chase had pulled out for her. "You haven't eaten, have you?"

"Well, no, but I didn't come by to eat. I can't stay very long. I really should be going soon."

"Nonsense." Suzanna pulled up a chair next to Ellie and patted her hand. "We can't possibly eat all this pizza. We'd love to have you join us." She paused and smiled at Chase. "I'm glad you came by, Mama. I've been wanting you to meet Chase for a long time, too."

Chase lowered his large frame to the modest-size bentwood chair across the table from Ellie. His presence, and his height, seemed to dominate the small kitchen. And yet, when he spoke to Ellie, he conveyed the singular message that he cared about her. It was a special quality of his. "Mrs. Schafer, I'm dying to know what happened on Thursday. And, I might add, I think you're a very courageous woman to invade the Rogues the way you did. I applaud your actions."

"You do?" Ellie's facial expression changed—ever so slightly.

"I certainly do."

"I'm surprised you even knew about it." She looked accusingly at Suzanna.

"Mama, it wasn't exactly a secret. Half the town knew. The female half, anyway. Of course, I told Chase. I was very concerned about you."

Ellie's blue eyes snapped at her daughter. "And you were worried about your job. I told you it would be all right."

"But your defiance *was* a surprise." Suzanna lifted a wedge of pizza. "Can I serve you?"

"Well, maybe I'll have just one little slice." Ellie took a sip of her drink.

"This smells great, Suzanna. Thanks." Chase gave her a fond look as he transferred a pizza slice to his plate.

Suzanna acknowledged his comment with a little smile. Ellie would have to be blind to miss the obvious affection in his tone as he rhapsodized over her store-bought pizza. Oh, well. She didn't care. She helped herself.

"Now, tell me what happened at the Rogues lunch." Chase looked from Ellie to Suzanna with sincere interest.

"You should have seen Mama, Chase!" Suzanna launched into the story first. "She looked so spiffy in her new navy-and-white suit. And, the most amazing thing happened. Half the ladies in town, including some members' wives, encouraged her, every step of the way."

"They knew about it?"

"Oh, my, yes!" Ellie said. "That was half the fun." Her blue eyes twinkled. "The other half was countering Don Rutherford. You should have seen his face."

Chase hooted with laughter. "I'd have given my eye teeth to be there. But only as an observer, not as a member."

Ellie giggled. "He was so mad, his face was purple!"

"But what about O'Hara?"

"Actually, he wasn't so bad."

"Then, he did listen to you?"

Ellie nodded. "After Suzanna's speech, I saw my chance to speak to Mr. O'Hara. I told him that we needed his story for Wordsworth, which is our library's oral county-history project. When I explained our purpose and how we record the histories, he thought it was a great idea. I'd just given him my name and number on a slip of paper when Don spotted me. Before Mr. O'Hara had a chance to say a thing to me, he boomed out, 'Madam, you do not belong on these premises!'"

"Oh, no, Mama!" Suzanna's heart went out to her mother. "Were you embarrassed?"

"At first I was, when the whole place got dead quiet and everybody stared at me. But then Mr. O'Hara said, 'Rutherford, this lady and I were having a private conversation before you interrupted.' And to me he said, 'I'd be proud to be a part of your history. My secretary will be in touch with you to set up a time. You have my word.' I knew I had accomplished my mission. So even when Rutherford escorted me out, I was floating on air!"

"This will make a great story for the histories, too, Mrs. Schafer," Chase encouraged seriously. "I hope you're going to record it."

"Why, Mr. Clements, I never thought of it."

"You definitely should. You're an important player in the history of this county. This is a monumental event. And I'm proud to know you."

"Oh, go on, Mr. Clements. It was nothing much," Ellie replied modestly, dabbing her mouth with her napkin.

"Don't underestimate what you've done, Mrs. Schafer. You've shaken the bones of this community. People will be talking about this for years. They may as well get the facts right." He reached for another wedge of pizza. "And please, call me Chase. Not many people in this town call me Mr. Clements."

Ellie grinned, obviously taken with the man. "Okay, Chase."

"I think he's right, Mama," added Suzanna. "You belong in Grace County history!"

"Hmm. It might be worthwhile...if things turn out," Ellie mumbled thoughtfully.

"You should have seen her at the end, Chase." Suzanna picked up the story. "Old Man Rutherford escorted her into my office and before he could even start in on the whole thing being my fault, Mama called him 'Don' and proceeded to pin his ears back."

"I'm impressed, Mrs. Schafer." Chase's dark eyes shone with admiration. "You took on one of the bigwigs of this town. And won!"

"I had a little edge." Ellie pinched a bit of crust and smiled impishly. "You see, Don and I go way back. To schooldays. In fact, he asked for my hand before your father did, Suzanna. But I held out for Miles. I knew all along he was a better man. And I never regretted it for a minute."

"Mama!" Suzanna leaned back, aghast. "You mean Old Man Rutherford could have been my daddy?"

Chase chuckled. "The world turns in strange circles, doesn't it? I think you made the far better choice, Mrs. Schafer."

Suzanna shook her head. "Well, I was impressed with the way you handled my boss, Mama. Now, if only Mr.

O'Hara keeps his word, the whole thing will be a complete success. And no harm done."

"Oh, he did. Or, at least, his secretary did. Late this afternoon. We set up an appointment for next week."

"Congratulations," Chase said.

"That's great, Mama!" Suzanna hugged her mother joyously. "I'm so proud of you!"

"That's what I stopped by to tell you. That and . . ." Ellie stood and tucked her chair neatly under the table. "The fact that I've decided to apply for membership in the Rogues Club."

10

"MAMA! YOU CAN'T do that!"

"Why not?"

"Why, because..." Suzanna sputtered. "Because you shouldn't. You got what you wanted. Why can't you leave them alone now?"

"Because what they're doing isn't right, Suzanna," Ellie explained sweetly.

Suzanna stared at her mother. She could hardly believe her ears. Who would ever imagine that this gentle, domestic woman would turn into a feminist? "But Mr. O'Hara has set up a meeting with you for Wordsworth. Isn't that enough?"

"No. This has nothing to do with Mr. O'Hara and Wordsworth. This is a matter of principle. I don't think the men should be exclusive in this town. Do you? It's unfair to the women."

"No, but ... lots of things are unfair in this world, Mama. Tackle one of *them!*"

Ellie raised her eyebrows. "Maybe I will. But first, I believe in cleaning up my own backyard."

"Oh, brother!" Suzanna groaned and hid her face in one hand. "This is great. Just great!"

"I'm surprised at you, Suzanna. I thought you'd be glad I got out of my rocking chair and started doing something worthwhile. At the very least, I expected you to be supportive. All the dear girls are behind me one hundred percent. They're going to help me launch a campaign."

"The 'dear girls'? A 'campaign'?" Suzanna had visions of her mother and her lady friends marching through town holding banners: Freedom for Women! Join the Rogues!

"My friends—the Crazy Quilters and the ladies working on the Wordsworth committee—all plan to support me. Especially since my own daughter is against me."

"I'm not against you, Mama. I just don't understand why you have to tackle this now."

"The time is right, Suzanna. Changes are being made. It's high time the Rogues made the most important change of all. Their membership." She started to put on her coat, and Chase was immediately on his feet to help her.

"You're right about timing, Mrs. Schafer," he agreed. "You can use yesterday's incident as a starting place."

"Thank you, Chase." Ellie adjusted her coat and turned to Suzanna. "Can't you see that the Rogues is a good ole boys' club that excludes women in business, as well as membership?"

"And nonmembers," Chase added.

Suzanna looked from her mother to Chase. They were as different as daylight and dark, yet they were obviously united on this issue. "Yes, I suppose...." They were right, and she knew it. She just didn't think her job at the Rutherford Country Club could stand the rigors of such a campaign.

"I hope when you've had a chance to think about it, you'll come around, Suzanna." Ellie tucked her purse into the crook of her arm.

"Oh, Mama . . ." The way Ellie looked as she stood there, with her coat buttoned up fastidiously and her hands clasped primly, she could be anybody's innocuous, sweet-faced mother. Instead, she had turned into an activist. Suzanna felt as if the metamorphosis in her mother had taken place almost overnight.

"Thanks for dinner. The pizza was very good. It was nice to meet you, Chase." Ellie shook his hand formally.

"I'm behind you all the way, Mrs. Schafer." He also extended his left hand over hers and patted it. "I think what you're doing is long overdue. If I can help in any way, let me know."

"Thank you, Chase. I need all the bipartisan support I can get. I'll let you know." She turned to go.

"Mama . . . wait." Suzanna stood. "I . . . I won't abandon you in this, Mama. I do think the Rogues' methods are unfair and change is probably overdue. I may not promote what you're doing, but I won't work against you in any way."

Ellie blinked a couple of times. "Thanks. I certainly never intended to do anything to risk your job, Suzanna. This whole thing just happened and seemed to get beyond me. Do you understand? I hope it'll be all right for you."

"Of course, I do. I'm probably worrying for nothing." She hugged Ellie and walked her to the door. When she returned, Suzanna slumped into a chair. "I hope I'm worrying for nothing."

"Is your job that valuable, Suzanna?"

She looked at Chase defiantly. "Is taking care of my son valuable? We have to eat, don't we?"

"The obvious answer to that is yes. But do you have to compromise your principles in order to provide for your son?"

"Until tonight, I wasn't aware of compromising anything."

"Okay, Suzanna, I won't argue that point. But you wanted your mother involved in something beyond herself, and now she is. It's something pretty great, in fact. And still, you aren't satisfied."

"Well, it's not exactly what I had in mind."

"No. You want the world—especially your mother—to function within your guidelines. It doesn't always turn out that way."

"So far, nothing is working the way I want."

"Nothing? Not even us?"

She sighed. "Slipping around isn't my idea of a perfect relationship."

"Then, let's stop it."

She stared at him for a long minute. "I...don't know, Chase."

"Obviously you aren't ready, if you're that hesitant."

She looked down at her hands. "I'm sorry, Chase. There are just too many things happening in my life right now. I can't stand more stress-inducing action."

"You mean something else that might impact on your job."

She nodded. "I guess."

"Then, let's leave well enough alone. For now. I don't mind slipping around. I find it sort of exciting."

"The man of my secret fantasy..." Softly she touched his cheek with gentle fingertips. "I wish it could be different."

"My fantasy is about to come true."

"What's that?"

"In bed with you all night and into the morning."

She laughed, somewhat embarrassed. "This is a business trip. Just how romantic is Little Rock?"

"As romantic as we make it. You might be surprised. They have preserved history, great museums, a beautiful park, the Arkansas River, a private bedroom somewhere . . . Sounds romantic to me."

"We'll be staying at the Capital Hotel."

"Ahh, very beautiful bedrooms. And Rutherford is paying for this? I love it!" Chase chuckled mockingly.

"I will have to make an appearance at the seminar, you know."

"Of course. It's the private time that I'm looking forward to."

"Me, too." She squeezed his hand. "I'm glad Mama got to meet you tonight, Chase. Really."

"I'm surprised. I expected you to steer her in another direction."

"Why?"

"Oh, most women don't want me to meet their mother. And the way we've been slipping around, I thought you'd feel the same."

"Chase, I . . . I'm not ashamed of you. It's just that with the way Rutherford feels about you, our relationship could present some problems right now."

"It's okay. I think Ellie and I could be friends."

"Obviously. She's got a cause that you can support."

"You have a remarkable mother, Suzanna. She's tackling something very important—actually, something bigger than us, bigger than your job. Maybe not more important to you, but greater in the whole scheme of things. This is about equal rights."

"I know." Suzanna shook her head, still astonished at the changes in Ellie. "My mother *is* amazing. When I first arrived back here, she was a sweet little ole lady gossiping with her friends at quilting parties. Then she was encouraged by her friends, whom she calls 'the dear girls,' to break a taboo with the fifty-year-old all-male Rogues Club. Now she wants to be one of the boys!"

"I wouldn't put it past her, either. Equal rights finally is coming to Grace. I love it!" Chase laughed and brought her hand to his lips. "Your mother has a remarkable daughter, too. Beautiful in all ways. But, a bit of a worrywart." He kissed her fingers individually. "I'd be proud to accompany you to Little Rock, if you promise not to worry about what hasn't happened yet and what may not ever happen and to simply enjoy our time together."

Suzanna considered the proposition with a blithe smile. "Okay, it's a deal. Two days and two nights— carefree and fun."

"Especially the nights." He kissed her fingertips. "But I'm betting on the mornings."

SUZANNA KEPT HER DEAL with Chase. From the moment they left Grace in the heavily wooded Ozarks, she was determined to make their trip enjoyable. They chatted spiritedly, and a bit nervously, on the journey to Little Rock. But when they stepped into the spectacular, stained-glass-domed lobby of the Capital Hotel, a strange thing began to happen.

The move to another place seemed to transform their relationship as a couple. There was no more hiding; no need for it since no one knew them. Their pasts and reputations didn't matter. They could be openly affectionate and endearingly romantic. No one paid attention to them.

Suzanna thrived in Chase's company, and her face was aglow with love as she hooked on to his arm. This was a different Chase: one she'd never seen, but one she loved even more.

As if the change of location from rural to urban flipped a page in his "how-to-dress-and-act" book, Chase revealed another side to the complicated man Grace called a "river rat." Gone were the jeans and boots. Instead, he wore slacks, perfectly tailored, and shiny leather loafers. The plaid shirts with thermal underwear showing at the neck were replaced by pastel, button-down oxford shirts and an exquisite fawn-colored suede jacket. To Suzanna he was magnificent.

She proudly walked beside Chase, feeling as if she were floating a few inches above the plush carpet of the hotel lobby. Their room had been elegantly restored to its original Victorian style, with marble-topped dressers and a four-poster bed.

But when the bellboy left, closing the door, she realized they were entirely alone, with no barriers to keep them apart. The heavily draped windows prevented anyone from seeing inside. The bed was empty and inviting; Chase was undoubtedly eager to get her there. And suddenly, she was as nervous as if they'd never made love.

She flung open her suitcase and began shaking her blouses and suits. "These will get wrinkled if I don't get them on hangers."

"Me, too." Chase did the same, adding several pairs of slacks to the rack beside her clothes. "I brought a tie." He laughed and held it up for her to see.

She wrinkled her nose. "Need some help picking out one that matches?"

"Doesn't it match?"

"Not the browns you brought."

"Oh. Well, yes, I guess I do need some help." He turned to her, pulling her slowly, purposefully into his arms. "Suzanna, can't you tell that I need you in more ways than you think?"

"Chase, I know this sounds silly, but—"

"You don't have to say it. I know. We need some time." He kissed her forehead and embraced her in a comfortable hug. "Let's check out this place. Take a walk, have a drink, relax."

She rested her head against his chest and sighed. "You must think—"

"Hold it." He gripped her shoulders with both hands. His dark eyes were piercing but sincere. "It doesn't matter what I think. Your feelings are honest. And I would never misinterpret them or tell you to change."

"Chase, you're remarkable."

"No, I'm real." He grinned and a teasing glint lit his eyes. "Anyway, we didn't come here for a sexual orgy. We have that at home!"

"Why, you—" She lunged playfully for him, but he caught her in his arms.

He kissed her quickly, then took her hand, and they ran laughing from the room. They found an intimate nook on the hotel's columned mezzanine beneath the stained-glass ceiling and ordered cocktails. Inspired by the romantic sounds of a piano in the background, they began to talk in more detail about their pasts.

Suzanna revealed for the first time what life really had been like with Zack. How she and Ross had moved willingly at first, how she'd kept hoping for marriage, how he'd kept promising.

Chase felt himself grow angry about the way Zack had treated Suzanna, especially after she'd had his child and given up everything to follow him. "And what was the final, deciding factor that made you want to leave him?"

"Actually, Ross and I hadn't lived with him for quite a while. He went to Wyoming on some temporary job or other, and we stayed in Louisiana so Ross could continue at one school. There was a series of events that led me to leave, apart from the fact that Zack and I basically had no real relationship anymore. My father's death was a hard blow. And I felt bad that my family hardly knew Ross. He didn't know them at all, of course. When I went back to Louisiana after the funeral, I realized that I was no longer close to either Zack or my family. So what the heck was I doing there?"

"Is that when you decided to return to Grace and look for a job?"

"Well . . . employment was a big problem because I had a very good job managing a hotel and convention center in Lafayette." She chuckled. "I actually had a good boss and great working conditions. I hated to leave it. But when Mama told me Mr. Rutherford was looking for a manager to get the new country club started, the opportunity was too good to miss."

"Your mother was thrilled when she found out you were coming back. She told everybody in town."

"I'll bet." Suzanna rolled her eyes.

"Even *I* heard you were coming, and I'm not in the mainstream."

"Now that I know about her and Old Man Rutherford, I'm sure she had some influence on his willingness to interview me. Otherwise, he never would have picked up my résumé and called me."

"Ellie knew that once he met you, he'd have to recognize your skills and abilities."

Suzanna shrugged. "I do have the work experience that he needed for this job."

"I'm sure it wasn't easy to find someone with your skills in Grace." Chase nodded. "Your mother is very wise. She knew what it would take to get her daughter back—a decent job. So she went after it."

"You know, you're right." In retrospect, Suzanna could see how Ellie must have worked behind the scenes. "All that time, I thought she was sitting at home, making quilts."

"Ellie is quite a woman."

"I feel the same about your mother, Chase, even though I never met her. It took a strong, self-assured woman to do what she did. Not only was taking care of Darlene's child unpopular, it must have been difficult for her."

Chase nodded, tight-lipped. "Especially when Darlene ran off, and Mama got sick."

"I don't really know what happened, just the rumors." She reached out and took his hand, cradling it in her lap. "But I'll bet you took care of them both."

His face seemed to grow darker, more shadowed, as he remembered those difficult days. "There was no one else. My dad had gone by then. And it was damned tough. I'm not the nurse type, but she was so sick, and we had no money for help. I had no choice but to care for her. And what did I know about little kids?"

"How old was Ken?"

"About three." He hesitated, remembering that awful year. "But, you know, my mother and I grew closer during that time. She taught me a lot then."

"Taught you?"

"Well, I'd never been one to listen much before that. I was always on the run or fighting with my old man. When she finally had me there all the time, she taught me about being honest, and accepting myself and—" he paused and grinned shyly "—how to cook, especially for a growing boy. She knew those were things I'd be needing. And she was right."

Suzanna squeezed his hand and blinked back the tears. This man who was as tough as nails and twice as hard, had a tender streak. It was buried deep, but two people had been able to penetrate his stony facade. She hoped she could be the third. "Yes, your mother was very special, Chase." *And so are you.*

They finished their drinks, then dined on seafood at Ashley's, the hotel's four-star restaurant. Later Suzanna tried to blame her boldness on the wine, but deep down, she knew it came from her heart. She just didn't want to lose him. Ever.

And Chase loved every moment, even though he pretended to be astonished.

This time, when they entered their luxurious hotel room, Suzanna wasn't nervous at all. She knew what she wanted and proceeded to go after it. *After him*. Someone had already turned the bed down, leaving a chocolate mint on the top pillow. All that was lacking was the loving couple.

Humming, she turned down the lights, then found a radio station that played jazz. Chase's eyes were still adjusting to the semidarkness when she kicked off her basic-black pumps. He turned to watch as she discarded her business suit. By then she was swaying to the music and unbuttoning her blouse.

Chase grinned, hands on hips. This was not a show to be missed. With teasing deliberation Suzanna discarded her silk shirt and shimmied out of her slip. With sweeping motions of arms and legs, she stripped off her dark panty hose. As she continued to hum with the music and sway in her own sensual way, she removed her bra and panties.

At this point, Chase applauded her efforts. "All right!"

"I'm not finished," she warned, sidling up to him with a tiny mint chocolate between her lips. And that was how she fed him his half—their lips touching, nibbling, tasting.

Then, with swift, sure fingers she unbuttoned his shirt, quickly exposing his chest. She placed several moist kisses on its muscled surface while her hands sought his zipper. He was hard already, and she cooed her approval in sexy, whispered tones.

Just when he thought he could no longer just stand there while she caressed him, she murmured something about the bed. Patiently helping him out of his shoes, socks and slacks, she pushed him back onto the cool sheets.

Instantly, Suzanna straddled him and proceeded to become the most erotic lover that he'd ever known. She succeeded in replacing any and all dreams he had of them making love. *She* was better by far than any fantasy. Her silken flesh moved smoothly over him, driving him to distraction, until finally she took him completely. Her kisses were fierce; her body motions, frantically rhythmic, causing a jolting climax to radiate through his entire body.

When the waves of his passion began to recede, he became intensely aware of Suzanna. The sight of her still astride him was enough to make him hard again. He watched her gyrations with satisfaction.

Her head was back, her eyes closed. Her pink lips formed an O and, with a series of little moans, she arched her back and rode to ecstasy. When it was over, she slumped down over his outstretched body as if she wanted to pin him to the bed. They lay like that for a long time.

Eventually he wrapped his arms around her and rolled them over so that she was on her back, looking up at him with sultry, half-closed eyes. "We were great together, weren't we?"

"Yes," she murmured with a sleepy smile and, closing her eyes, she nestled in the curve of his strong body.

He trailed a string of kisses across her cheek, ending at her earlobe. "What are you trying to prove?"

She raised her head and kissed his jutting chin. "I want you to know that you won't find a better lover. Anywhere."

"I'll concede that without question. But I'm not looking for another."

"Chase, I don't want to lose you."

"What? I never thought I'd hear such a thing from you, Suzanna."

"You are the best of everything I've ever known. Best friend. Best man." She traced his nose with her finger. "Best lover."

He stroked her cheek. "I've never been called the best of anything. The worst, yes."

"But they don't know the Chase that I do. The caring man. The loving son. The good father." She moved his hand to cover one of her bare breasts. "The excellent lover."

"Suzanna . . ." He kissed her fervently.

"Chase, don't leave me."

"Never. I'd be a fool to try to escape this. You're the only woman who's ever taken me to her bed and never tried to change me."

"I like you, just this way." She ran her hand down his side and stopped at his thigh.

Quivering with pleasure, he kissed her again. "And I like you, just like this, right here, all night, till morning."

They curled in each other's arms and slept until the pale light of a new day woke them. Slowly, sweetly, without the feverish frenzy of the previous times, they made love again.

"This is what mornings are for," he whispered in her ear.

SUZANNA ATTENDED the morning seminars, but spent the afternoons with Chase. Hand in hand, they walked the tree-lined paths of Riverfront Park beside the Arkansas River. They toured the restored historic district and bought each other little gifts in Market Place.

In the midst of their excursion, Chase hailed a cab and, without revealing their destination, took her to the Fox Orchids greenhouses. There he presented her with a spectacular blue orchid. "Its beauty compares only to yours, m'love," he proclaimed formally.

She smiled. "You are such a romantic."

When they could keep from touching each other no longer, they hurried back to the hotel, where they made love wildly, passionately.

"I'm sorry this is the last night. I wish we could stay the weekend," she told him later.

He whispered, "We'll have to double our pleasures tonight." Then he kissed her neck until she writhed all over the bed.

The next morning they made love again—another sample of what life could be like if they lived together. But, as far as Suzanna could see, they couldn't consider that option.

She attended the final session of the seminar while Chase packed and prepared for their noon checkout. When she returned, Chase was standing at the window, his back to her.

She gazed over the stack of luggage in the center of the floor. "Looks like everything's done. Are you ready to go, Chase?"

"Yeah." His voice was gravelly and low.

She halted. It didn't even sound like Chase. He stood with his hands in his pockets, not even turning around to greet her. He'd been so warm and wonderfully affectionate during their time alone that this sudden indifference seemed totally unlike him.

Suzanna looked around with regret. Their room had been the site of a blossoming intimacy. They'd revealed all their passions and feelings to each other, held nothing back. They'd grown infinitely closer.

Sliding her arms around his waist, she laid her head against his back. "I hate to leave, too. This has been a wonderful time, Chase. I've enjoyed every minute."

"Me, too." He pressed his hands to hers. They were cold and clammy. "But I've got to get back as soon as possible."

"Chase, is anything wrong?" When he didn't answer, she moved around to face him. "What is it?"

His face was dark and shadowy. His expression, grim. "I got a call from Bo this morning. Darlene's back."

"Ken's mother? She's at the Boon Docks?" Suzanna drew in a slow breath. She had no way of knowing what this could mean, but Chase's expression told her he was very worried. "Well, let's get on the road."

11

A WEEK LATER, Suzanna pulled to a stop behind an unfamiliar, mud-caked white pickup in Chase's driveway.

"Whose truck is *that?*" Ross asked.

"It must be the, uh, one that brought Ken's mother." Darlene and her boyfriend were still there, sleeping until noon and generally making Chase's life miserable. Suzanna was proud of him, though, for he was enduring patiently. He had something greater at stake than his own discomfort: Ken.

"Gosh, I'm surprised that thing runs!" Ross commented. "What a wreck! Chase would *never* let his truck look like that!"

"You're right, Ross. He has too much pride in himself."

"And his truck." Ross grabbed the door handle.

Suzanna grasped his arm before he could get out. "Please, don't say anything about that truck's condition."

"Sure, Mom." He tried to pull away, but she held him another moment.

"And don't ask questions about Ken's mother. You and I can talk about it later if you want to know anything." Suzanna didn't expect to know any more about Darlene later than she did now, but she wanted to communicate openly with her son.

Ross rolled his eyes. "All right. Can I go now?"

She nodded and released his arm.

"Come on, Mom! I'll bet Ken's waiting!" He lurched from the car and dashed across the lawn.

Suzanna followed more slowly. Chase had been to their cottage several times during the week, mostly late at night. And he had spent a good deal of the time expressing to her his growing frustration with the life Darlene had made for herself, and with Darlene's inability to see through the aimlessness of her boyfriend. At the heart of it, Suzanna knew, was his deep fear that his sister would take Ken with her when she left.

Suzanna would have preferred to stay out of the difficult family situation, but Chase had insisted that he wanted her to meet Darlene. So she'd agreed to bring Ross over this Saturday. Bo and Wiley Jessup, Darlene's boyfriend, planned to work on the houseboat. The boys were to help with the project, but Suzanna suspected they were just curious to see the underside of a houseboat and wanted to play around the river.

She approached Chase's house hesitantly. She'd tried to explain to Ross that Darlene was Ken's biological mother, just as Zack was his own biological father; and that Chase was actually Ken's uncle, although he took care of him and loved him as a father would. It was complicated for a kid to understand—even complicated for her.

But she couldn't answer Ross's most poignant, childlike question. "If she's Ken's real mother, then why doesn't she live with him?"

Suzanna's "I don't know" answer was, she realized, inadequate. She only hoped Ross wouldn't pursue the issue by asking embarrassing questions today.

Chase met her at the door with a grateful smile and a quick kiss. "Hi. Glad you came. Darlene's up now, so you can meet her." He led Suzanna toward a young woman sitting on the sofa. "Darlene, this is Suzanna Schafer. You remember her, don't you?"

Darlene pushed her pale, tousled hair back and drawled, "Sure do." She took a big puff on her cigarette before putting it in the ashtray on the coffee table. "Hi, Suzanna. We go way back, don't we?"

"Yes, we certainly do, Darlene. It's nice to see you again."

"You look terrific, Suzanna. But you always were pretty." Darlene crossed shapely, bare legs and pulled her tattered chenille robe over them. "I like your hair that way—shorter on one side."

Suzanna took a chair. "It's great to see you again, Darlene. The last time must have been high school."

"Yeah. I was probably pregnant. And you were going with that blond hunk—what was his name?" She snapped her fingers. "Oh, yeah, Zack. Whatever happened to him?"

"He's, uh—actually, I don't know. Haven't seen him in a couple of years."

"Coffee, Suzanna?" Chase was already halfway to the kitchen. He was obviously uncomfortable around his sister. Everything she said and did offended him. Now Suzanna could see why. And yet there was something likable about Darlene, too.

When Suzanna hesitated, Darlene spoke up. "I'll take a refill, please, Chase."

"Only half a cup for me, thanks," Suzanna replied. "I've already had several cups." She could see that Darlene had just gotten out of bed and was having her morning coffee. And cigarette. The boyfriend wasn't in sight, and Suzanna assumed that he was already working on the boat with Bo. She soon discovered that her assumption was wrong.

Chase returned with a cup of coffee for Suzanna and poured more for Darlene. "I'm going to take the boys down to the river where Bo's working on the boat."

"Go ahead and wake Wiley," Darlene said to Chase. "I know you're dying to."

"It's after ten." Chase looked at his watch out of habit. "I'm sure Bo's already started, and I—"

"You don't have to explain to me, Chase. Go ahead, do it. Wiley can't be bumming around here forever."

"He said he wanted to work on the boat."

Darlene set her coffee cup down with a bang. "If you don't wake him, I will!"

Chase returned to the kitchen. Suzanna had never seen him like this—so edgy and snappy. And she was amazed at the differences between Chase and Darlene. She also couldn't believe what he tolerated from his sister. Was this the same arrogant, headstrong man she admired so much? She heard him talking to the boys in the back room, explaining why they were going to be a little late.

This Chase was definitely different. This was a man who loved a little boy and, at the moment, feared losing him. She understood but could only listen sympathetically and stand by helplessly. Maybe he felt the same way: helpless.

Suzanna chatted with Darlene about her work at the country club. Darlene ran down a list of at least ten jobs she'd had this year alone. And now, once again, she was jobless because they were on their way out west; Wiley wanted to try his hand at being a cowboy.

"When are you supposed to be there?" Suzanna asked carefully.

"Oh, sometime before spring. That's when they round up the range cattle. Wiley even bought a hand-tooled, leather saddle in Kansas City. He was so excited about that saddle." Darlene giggled. "Just like a little kid. He can't wait to use it on a real horse."

"Hmm." Suzanna could hear Wiley cursing like a sailor when Chase woke him. Tactfully, she tried to carry on a conversation with Darlene as if nothing were happening in the background. "So, do you want to be a cowgirl, Darlene?"

"Me?" Darlene lit another cigarette. "Heavens, no! I'll probably get a job as cook on the ranch. Or I could waitress in the nearest town."

Chase ushered the boys to the living-room door. "I'm taking them down to the river with Bo. Want to come along, Suzanna?"

She stood. Seeing his expression, she definitely wanted to go with him. He was furious.

Darlene gestured impatiently. "Oh, Chase, wait on Wiley. He'll be out in a few minutes."

"No, Darlene. I don't want him cursing like that around the boys. I don't need his help that badly."

"He's just a little grumpy in the mornings," she explained. "He'll be all right after he's had a cup of coffee."

"Sorry, no." Chase shook his head. "I'd rather not. Anyway, I want to check on the boat's condition myself. See you later."

He opened the door and practically pushed everyone out, including Suzanna. Behind them, she could hear Darlene's whine. "Chase Clements, you're such a stubborn jerk. If you'll wait—"

He closed the door and motioned for the boys to get in his pickup. Sensing his agitation, they hurried toward the shiny, clean truck.

Suzanna took Chase's hand and walked rapidly to keep up with him. He didn't look at her, just kept his gaze straight ahead. His lips were clamped tightly together. A muscle in his jaw flexed. *This* was the man she loved. A rugged, complex, tender-tough man with a temper that he was now suppressing.

The boys piled into the cab of the truck, and Suzanna turned to Chase. "You're doing the right thing, Chase. I know it's hard, but you must be patient."

"I'd like to tell her—" He stopped in midsentence and shook his head. "I just hope she has sense enough to do what's right for Ken. I'd hate to have a legal fight with my own sister, but I'd do it to keep that kid."

Suzanna squeezed his hand. "I think she'll do what's right for her child. Most mothers would."

"Darlene's not like most mothers," he grated through tight lips.

"You'd be surprised, Chase."

"You're damn right, I would be."

THE NEXT WEEK, on the day before Thanksgiving, Suzanna arrived at Ellie's house with Ross. The plan was for him to spend the night with his Gramma and help her make pies and get ready for the family holiday gathering. Suzanna had a proposal to make that she wasn't sure Ellie would go along with, but she had to give it a shot. It was important to her, and to her relationship with Chase.

As they approached the front door, the rhythm of drums could be heard radiating loudly from the usually quiet home.

"What's Gramma up to now?"

Suzanna grinned at Ross. "Sounds like rock music to me."

"Yep. 'Mony Mony,'" Ross confirmed and pounded on the door.

Ellie, dressed in bright purple tights, matching shorts, and a T-shirt that read Late Bloomers, swung open the door. Suzanna and Ross stared at her for a moment. Behind her were three more ladies of the same age, dressed similarly, and gyrating to the beat.

"Mama..." Suzanna struggled for words. "What, uh—"

"Suzanna, sugar, come on in. The dear girls and I have discovered Jazzercize! It's so much fun!"

"That's great, Mama." Suzanna found herself shouting in order to be heard. "But, uh, don't you think the music's a little loud?" The beat surged through the open door and drowned out normal speech.

"Gramma, can I go watch TV in the back room?"

Ellie hugged Ross and sent him off with a pat. She'd fixed up a room for him, complete with bunk beds and a little TV set. As a result, he was much more eager to visit her.

"Can we talk a minute, Mama?"

Ellie pulled Suzanna into the kitchen and closed the door, thus muffling the cacophony. "There. That's better, isn't it?"

"Yes, but I, uh . . ." It occurred to Suzanna that her mother looked like a gray-haired grape, but a darling one.

"Make it quick, sugar. I'm almost up to my aerobic heartbeat and don't want to lose it."

"Well, it's about Thanksgiving. . . ."

"Don't tell me you want to change the menu again. Julie is already thawing the turkey," she said, referring to Suzanna's sister-in-law. "I thought we gave you some easy dishes. There's nothing to making cranberry salad. And anybody can do stuffed celery."

"No, Mama." Suzanna shuffled uncomfortably. "Turkey's fine. The menu's great."

"Then, what is it?" Ellie propped her hands on her pudgy hips. "I've never seen you so fidgety. Aren't you coming?"

"I know how you want everyone together this year. And I want that, too, it's just that—"

"Spit it out, Suzanna!"

"I'd like to invite someone else."

"Well, sugar, you know I don't care if you invite someone else to share our Thanksgiving dinner. Is it a little friend of Ross's? Or yours?"

"Yes, Mama. Both."

"A man? Who is it?" Ellie grinned expectantly.

Suzanna took a deep breath. "Chase Clements. I'll bring extra food."

If Ellie had a reaction, she hid it beautifully. "And his young son, too?"

Suzanna could have hugged her mother. "Actually, no. Ken's mother, Darlene, is in town. And she and her, uh, boyfriend, are taking Ken to the Crater of Diamonds State Park for a few days."

"Over Thanksgiving?"

Suzanna nodded miserably. "Chase will be alone. So, I—"

Ellie put her hand on Suzanna's forearm. "You don't have to explain, sugar. I'm sure your reasons are solid. It's fine if you want to invite him."

Suzanna sighed a smile. "Thanks, Mama."

"Anyway, I like the man. He's got a good head on his shoulders." She grinned devilishly. "And he's handsome, in a way."

"He likes you, too, Mama. He really admires what you're doing with the Rogues."

"As I said, the man has a good head."

"You've certainly changed your opinion of him."

"We all change, Suzanna. Or we sit in our same ole rut."

"Well, no one could possibly accuse you of sitting in a rut!" Spontaneously she hugged her mother. "Now, I'll go so you can get back to your exercise, er, Jazzercize."

"The dear girls and I are working hard today so we can eat a piece of pumpkin pie tomorrow." She patted her tummy.

"Good idea. We should all do that, I'm sure."

"Suzanna?"

"Yes, Mama?"

"Do you like him?"

Suzanna stopped and looked at her mother. It was a straightforward question. And it deserved an honest answer. "Yes, Mama. I do. Most people don't know it, but he's a good man."

"A man to tie to?"

"Maybe."

Ellie studied her daughter's face seriously. But before she could ask another question, Suzanna whirled away.

"See you tomorrow, Mama! Thanks a bunch!"

Suzanna drove directly to Chase's. She had already decided that if her mother had refused to accept him or even had been hesitant for him to join their family, she would have opted to spend the holiday alone with him.

When she asked Chase's whereabouts at the Boon Docks, Bo talked with her for a few minutes, before sending her over to Bull Shoals Lake. She drove around until she spotted him, then parked and hiked over to the man sitting alone on the bank, studying the water. Chase looked so lonely and miserable, she wanted to embrace him and assure him that everything would be all right.

"Bo said I might find you here." She sat beside him on the grassy brown turf. When Chase didn't reply, she added, "Ross said Ken wasn't at school today. I figured they left early."

"Can you believe that she took him out of school for her own convenience? That's how stupid she is."

"Chase, it's important for a boy to spend time with his mother, especially when she isn't around much. You know he won't miss anything important this last day before the holiday."

"Can you believe they're camping out and searching for diamonds over the Thanksgiving weekend?"

"Just be grateful it's unusually warm this week. Actually, Chase, this will be a Thanksgiving Ken'll long remember."

"Yeah. Me, too."

"That's not a bad way for Ken to think of his mother."

"If she brings him back."

"Bo said you were worried about that."

"Did he also tell you that I'm in a lousy mood?"

"Yes." She scooted closer, so that their legs were touching. "He said to tell you that he supplied Ken with a slip of paper with both your names and phone numbers on it in case . . . Ken should need it."

"Great! If he's kidnapped, he can drop the note with a gas attendant in California and hope to be rescued." Chase slapped his thigh, then rubbed it nervously. "Rescued from his own mother? Fat chance!"

"Chase!" She grabbed his arm and shook it, trying to make him think clearly. "He did what he thought was best at the time. Bo's concerned, too. And so am I."

Chase took a deep breath and muttered a low curse. "I know. And I appreciate it. I just feel so . . . caught."

"And helpless. So do we. But at least Bo's doing something." She slid her hand into his. "It may not be much, but it's an effort."

Chase accepted her affectionate gesture but continued to stare sullenly at the glistening, crystal water.

"Chase, please don't turn away from me. I want to be your friend, your support."

"There's nothing you can do about my problem."

"Maybe not. But I can listen."

He gazed solemnly at her. The intent gray-blue eyes reflected caring and concern. And love. He could see it. She didn't have to say any more. Before he realized it, Chase was spilling his emotions to her. "Why did they have to go to that diamond crater now? What if they don't stop there? What if they just keep going west?"

"Can I give you some possible answers?"

He nodded.

"They're looking for diamonds because Wiley has dedicated his life to looking for ways to get rich quick, and discovering diamonds sounds like a great way to do that. They're going now before they head west. They took Ken because Darlene needs to do some fun things for her son. She wants him to have good memories of their times together. And he will." Suzanna continued with an encouraging little smile. "And they won't keep going west—because Bo persuaded Wiley to leave his saddle here, where it's safe, while they're using the back of the truck for camping."

"You're saying they'll come back just because of a saddle?" Chase looked at her like she was crazy.

She nodded. "Not just 'a saddle.' This one is hand-tooled leather. It costs a lot of money."

"How can you compare the value of a kid to a saddle?"

"I'm not. But Wiley would. That saddle is his pride and joy. With that beautiful saddle flung over his shoulder, he's a ready-made cowboy. It's been his dream. He wouldn't give it up now."

Chase studied her for a moment. "You're right about that. He does value it. So, you think they'll be back?"

"Yes, I do." She hoped her supposition was correct.

"Well, we should know in a couple of hours. Ken's supposed to call when he gets there." Chase slapped his thigh again. "Can you believe they're camping this time of year? Sleeping in the back of that damn truck! What if he gets sick from this?"

"Chase, don't borrow worry. Ken's a strong, healthy boy. He'll be okay. His mother will take care of him."

"Hell, his mother doesn't know how to take care of him!"

"She'll do all right, Chase."

"You seem to have more confidence in her than I do."

"Maybe I do. I see in Darlene a young woman who loves her kid but just can't take charge of her life enough to take care of him. So, she's letting the one who can care for him do it: you. That's not dumb. That's a good mother's instincts."

He lifted her hand to his lips. "Where did such a beautiful woman as you get such insight?"

"Experience is a hard-nosed teacher. I'm a mother. And I have some instincts about these things." She shifted to face him and reached inside his jacket to adjust his shirt collar, letting her fingers rub against the warm skin of his neck. "My instincts tell me that you have an empty house tonight. And possibly an empty bed, too?"

He gave her a how-could-you-question-it glare.

She gave him a smug smile. "Ross is at Mama's."

His dark eyes lit with a tiny bit of joy for the first time since she'd joined him. "You can't possibly know how hard it's been for me to give up my bed to Wiley and Darlene."

"I can imagine." She scooted her fingers around to the back of his neck and continued to caress. "I'll bet it's been so uncomfortable for you on that sofa. Poor baby," she cooed. "Would you like someone to keep you warm tonight?"

"Hmm, I'm beginning to like the idea." He accepted her kiss. "A lot."

"We could make some cranberry salad and stuffed celery for Thanksgiving. And tomorrow morning..."

"Ahh, mornings with you...my favorite time of day."

She trailed her lips sensually from his mouth to his earlobe. "And then, later tomorrow, we can go to Mama's for Thanksgiving dinner."

He pulled back. "Don't feel sorry for me just because everybody's left. I don't have to be entertained on Thanksgiving Day."

"I don't feel sorry for you, Chase. I talked with Mama and—"

"Thanks, but no." He shook his head firmly. "Suz, I appreciate it, but Thanksgiving Day dinners are reserved for nice families. And nice families don't want the likes of me there."

"I do."

"Well, I guess I've already pulled your reputation down along the river with mine."

"I have my own reputation, thank you. You know something?" She placed her hands on his chest. "Darlene was right. You are a stubborn jerk."

"Suz-anna..."

She framed his face with her hands and forced him to look at her. "Please, Chase. Go for me. Anyway, I need help with that cranberry salad. I have Mama's recipe, but..." She shook her head helplessly.

"Am I being used?"

"Yes!" She kissed him soundly, knowing that she'd chinked a hole in his armor. That's all she needed for now. "Oh, yes!"

That night they stayed busy making the cranberry salad and stuffed celery. Chase even made a pecan pie using one of his mother's recipes. They worked and waited until midnight for Ken's call. By then, Chase was ready to call the highway patrol and the National Guard. When the phone finally rang, he dived for it.

Suzanna held her breath and watched his expression change during the conversation from anxiety to concern to anger to patience to relief and finally to a father's joy.

He hung up and stared bleakly at her for a moment. "Well—?"

"They had engine trouble in that damned truck. They're heading for the Crater of Diamonds State Park camping ground now." Chase rolled back on the bed, laughing deliriously. "He ate two Big Macs for supper, and he's having a ball! Thank God!"

Joyously, Suzanna hugged him. "I'm so glad, Chase. But I knew that Darlene had more sense than to do anything that might be harmful to her son."

"How could you know it when I didn't?"

"I told you: instinct. Women know these things." Her lips captured his in a fervent kiss.

"What did I do . . ." he murmured when she finally pulled back ". . . before you came along to brighten my life?"

"You sat in the dark and worried alone."

"You're absolutely right. It was awful, too. No . . ."

She kissed him again. "Say it, Chase. No love. Not like this."

"I can't disagree . . ." His words were muffled by another long kiss—one that led to lovemaking.

THE NEXT DAY, Chase felt completely accepted by Suzanna's family. Either they were genuinely adaptable to her ways or she had schooled them thoroughly.

Eventually he decided the former was the case. He got along well with her brother, Butch. He discussed recipes with Butch's wife, Julie. Their two little girls were delightful, and he found them interesting and quite different from the "son" he was used to. And Ellie made a point of talking to him, making him feel especially welcome.

The sudden phone call as they were gorging on second helpings of pie came as a surprise to all, especially to Ellie. She answered it and conversed for a few minutes. When she returned to the family, she wore a strained expression.

"What is it, Mama?" Butch asked. "Anything wrong?"

Everyone looked up.

"That was Alec McNeil. He's the secretary for the Rogues Club. It was his job to tell me that they called a special meeting last night to discuss my membership application. And a vote was taken." She paused and looked around.

Suzanna stood. "And? What happened, Mama?"

Ellie was strangely calm over an issue that she had pursued with such diligence. "My membership was turned down."

Everyone groaned "Ohh" in disappointed unison.

"Why? What reason did they give?" Chase asked. "They have to give you a reason."

Ellie took her seat near him. "Alec said that I don't qualify."

"They're stating gender? That's discrimination."

"No, not because I'm a woman. Every member must make substantial civic contributions to the community. And they have a committee that evaluates them and approves or disapproves those contributions. Based on those criteria, they say that I don't qualify."

"What about Wordsworth?" he persisted.

"I guess that isn't enough." She shrugged, obviously feeling defeated.

"Oh, Mama, I'm sorry." Suzanna murmured sympathetically and put her arm around Ellie's shoulder. Secretly, though, she was breathing a sigh of relief that it was over.

Chase leaned forward, his elbows on his widespread knees. "That's ridiculous, Ellie! In all the years you've spent as a law-abiding, contributing citizen in this community, you haven't done as much as any one of those jackasses who sit on the 'elite' board? Utter nonsense! Sounds to me like that committee is a tool to keep undesirable members out."

"I agree, Mama," Butch said. "Their main function is to find something wrong."

Chase shook his head. "If I were you, Ellie, I'd get a lawyer. And call the news media. This may be unconstitutional."

Suzanna stared at Chase, horrified by his recommendations to her mother. If Ellie followed his advice, whether she won or not, it would surely mean the kiss of death for Suzanna's job.

12

THE COUNTRY CLUB had been open three days when Chase called her. His voice sounded terse. "They're leaving. Soon."

Suzanna felt a hitch in her throat. "Are they—?"

"No. Ken's staying."

Relief flooded her. "I'm so glad, Chase. Does Ken know?"

"I don't think he ever suspected that it was a possibility. This is his home. Darlene didn't say much. Just that he seemed so settled here, and she couldn't take care of him like this. Did I mind?" He chuckled mirthlessly. "Mind? She doesn't realize how much trouble she saved herself and 'wonderful Wiley'!"

"When are they going, Chase?"

"In an hour or so. Could you...would you like to say goodbye? Darlene asked about you."

"Of course. I'll be right over."

When she arrived, the men and Ken were loading the truck in a cold, misty rain. Chase gave her a grateful look. "Darlene's inside packing. Go on in."

Wiley, she noticed, was taking pains to wrap his precious saddle in plastic and a heavy tarp. She dashed into the living room where a fire crackled in the fireplace. She found Darlene in Chase's bedroom, stuffing clothes into a duffel bag. Suzanna's heart went out to her. This scene was so familiar.

"Darlene, can I help do anything?"

"No, thanks. There isn't much."

"We . . . we all hate to see you go."

"Chase doesn't."

"Yes, he does, actually. It's just been a little crowded around here. He isn't used to that."

"Yeah, I know." Darlene smiled and pushed her blond hair back. "It'll be better this way. They say two women can't run the same house. I guess that applies to men, too. Chase and Wiley didn't get along very well."

Suzanna wanted to tell Darlene that Chase would probably be glad to build her a house somewhere on the property if she'd just stay. But it wasn't her place to say that. "Where are you going?"

"Wiley got a real good job on a guest ranch in Arizona."

Suzanna nodded. Zack had been excited to work on a guest ranch, too. "A guest ranch, huh?" Darlene seemed pleased that Wiley had a job. *Any* job.

"They used to be called dude ranches, but now they're guest ranches. They're going to provide a place for us to live and one meal a day. If I help out in the kitchen, we'll get two meals."

This part was familiar, too. Suzanna remembered Zack giving her a similar pitch about the new job in Wyoming. But by then, she was disillusioned enough to know it was no place for her and Ross. And she'd never regretted that decision. "So, you both have jobs waiting?"

Darlene nodded, obviously pleased. "Wiley always wanted to go west. This is a great opportunity."

"And you, too? Is that what you want?"

"I want—" Darlene crammed the final shirt into the duffel "—to be with Wiley. I'd be just as happy in Arkansas, but Wiley can't get a job around here."

Suzanna wondered if he'd even tried. "Well, he certainly can't be a cowboy here."

"Right." Darlene forced a little laugh. In the background they could hear the dialogue from a familiar children's TV show. "I'm going to miss that. Ken and I watched *Leave It To Beaver* reruns every evening. It's dumb, but we laughed anyway."

"I know what you mean. I do the same with Ross."

"Ken will be better off staying here."

"I agree." Suzanna could see that Darlene was struggling with her decisions. That, too, was agonizingly familiar. She sat on the edge of the bed. "Darlene, I know a little of what you're going through."

Darlene looked away. "How could you know? Your life is so . . . settled."

"No, it isn't really." Although the country club had opened without a hitch, Suzanna felt that her job—and possibly her life in Grace—was perched on the edge of a precipice. But Darlene didn't know anything about that. "I'm satisfied, though, with the decisions I've made. I used to live as you do—going with the man I loved from state to state, following his dreams."

"Zack?"

Suzanna nodded. "Ross's father. He could never settle down. For a number of years, that didn't matter to me. But as I got older and Ross started growing up, it did. Then I had some tough decisions to make. And I had to live with them. Maybe someday you, and Wiley, will find what you want."

"Thanks for . . . understanding and . . . everything." Darlene turned around, a wavering smile playing around her lips. She looked on the verge of tears. "Take good care of my men, Suzanna. Chase is happier than I've ever seen him. And Ken's a good kid, better than either Chase or I ever were."

"Chase's very relieved that you're not taking Ken. He really loves that kid."

"I know. And Ken loves him back. I wouldn't take him away from Chase. Ever." She chuckled in an effort to retain control. "I do have that much sense."

"Thank you, Darlene." With that admission, Suzanna felt like crying herself. "Good luck."

"I'm glad you're here, Suzanna. My kid needs a steady home. And a good mom."

"Ken has a mom. You'll always be his mother, Darlene. And he'll always remember your special times together. No one can take that from him. Or replace you in his heart."

Wiley called Darlene's name from the front door.

"Think so?"

"I know so."

The two women hugged tightly. Darlene grabbed the duffel and left quickly. She hugged Chase and thanked him, but lingered with Ken. Suzanna could hear her making promises about calling and writing and that next summer he could come visit them on the ranch. Ken seemed enthusiastic. Suzanna hoped the promises weren't empty ones.

She stood on the porch with Chase. He draped his arm around her, and they waved as the dilapidated white pickup pulled out of the driveway in the rain. Ken waved and ran after the truck a little ways. Then he stopped and stood in the muddy road in the rain and waved until the vehicle disappeared over the next hill.

Suzanna wiped away a tear. "It's going to be all right."

Chase breathed a sigh of relief. "Yeah. Until next time."

"No. She won't take Ken away from you. Ever."

"Do you know something I don't? Or can you see inside Darlene's brain?"

"She told me. She sees that Ken is happy here. And that you're taking good care of him." Suzanna slipped her arm around his waist. "She's smarter than you think, Chase. And she loves Ken. She's just mixed up. It's tough to decide between your child and the man you love."

"*You* made it."

"It was very hard at the time."

"Any regrets?"

"None," she said confidently. "Look at all I gained."

He kissed the sleek hair at her temple. "Me, too. How about a cup of hot chocolate by the fire?"

"I can't stay long, but it sounds great." She smiled at him. "That would probably be good for Ken, too. I'm sure he's soaked and cold."

They went inside together. Ken followed soon. He changed his clothes, then joined them, sitting on the floor near Chase. Suzanna handed him a steaming mug of hot chocolate, and they quietly sipped their drinks, staring into the blazing fire, each of them lost in thought.

THE COUNTRY CLUB was a busy hub of excitement.

"Suzanna, no matter what happens, I want you to

know that I never dreamed of hurting your job here."
Ellie looked up at her daughter sincerely. "I helped you
get this one. I certainly wouldn't want to help you lose
it."

"I know, Mama. Don't worry about it. If it happens, it happens. I have skills. I can work anywhere."
Suzanna sounded more confident than she felt.

"I admire you, Suzanna. You're so self-confident."

"And I admire your spunk, Mama. You're doing
something that most of us wouldn't have the nerve to
do."

"I've had lots of encouragement from my friends.
And my family," she added with a little grin. Both of
them knew that she'd received far more encouragement from friends than from family. "Is Chase coming
tonight?"

"Oh, yes. He's getting the boys settled. Bo has agreed
to help Ross and Ken with math homework." Suzanna
glanced toward the etched-glass door where several of
Ellie's "dear girls" were entering.

"Good. He's my main man." She gestured to the
dark-suited man standing nearby, chatting with someone. "Except for Barclay, of course."

"Barclay?"

"My lawyer, Barclay Edelstein," Ellie explained, as
if Suzanna should know the barrister by his first name.
"Actually, Chase is behind this whole thing. He's the
one who first pointed out how unfair the Rogues are."
Ellie turned to receive hugs and reassurances from her
friends.

Suzanna walked away, shaking her head. She'd have
to remember to thank Chase for all this, sometime.

The central lobby of the country club was filling up fast. Word had gotten around that the Rogues Club was resisting the female membership of a sweet-faced grandmother type. It made great news.

Ellie sat next to her lawyer, who had suggested that the more publicity she received, the better her chances. So Ellie had agreed to every request she'd had for an interview during the past few weeks.

Tonight, the Rogues had called a special session to reconsider Ellie's membership application. The scuttlebutt was that they were being pressured into admitting her. A possible lawsuit was pending if they refused her again. And they could be assured that any publicity the all-male club received would be negative.

Meanwhile Suzanna pretended that this was a social function, making sure the giant coffeepots were kept full and the large silver serving trays were replenished with finger sandwiches. It kept her too busy to think about the probable consequences.

Two television-news teams were setting up cameras in the corners of the room. Suzanna spotted at least a dozen reporters with notepads and tiny tape recorders. And, as people kept coming in, she figured half the town must be attending. At least half the female population was there.

A hush settled over the crowd as the Rogues Club members began to file in. Some of them were quite surprised at the crowd gathered to await the outcome of the vote. Alec was among the first to enter. He nodded politely to Ellie. Then he spotted Suzanna and moved toward her, obviously feeling some sort of obligation to speak.

"Hello Alec." She smiled gaily. "How's this for publicity? We didn't have a bigger crowd on opening day."

He scratched his head. "Beats me, Suzanna. Your mother sure has stirred up a hornet's nest."

"Yes, she has." On the tip of her tongue was an avowal that she had nothing to do with her mother's bold endeavors. But at this point, she was rooting for Ellie's successful acceptance into the club. "Mama is going to set this town back on its complacent ear."

"Think so, huh?"

Suzanna gestured grandly at the room. "How many women do you know who could do this?"

"Not many," he admitted. "Thank goodness."

"You know something, Alec?" Suzanna folded her arms. "These people are here because Mama's doing something that should have been done long ago."

"You think it's time we admitted women to the club?"

"High time, Alec."

"Maybe you're right. We'll know soon enough." Alec patted her arm and headed for the upstairs meeting room.

"Yes, we certainly will," Suzanna murmured with a growing confidence.

Mr. Rutherford entered next, surveying the crowd, then settling his angry gaze on Suzanna. Clamping down on this ever-present cigar, he made his way toward her. "What the hell's going on here?"

"You have to admit, it's pretty good publicity for the country club," she responded lightly.

"Harrumph," he grumbled. "It's crazy, that's what it is. I don't know why in the world your mother is doing all this. She certainly has changed since you came back to town, Suzanna."

"It's not my—" Suzanna halted in midsentence. She could feel her blood heating. Dammit! She wouldn't defend her mother or herself to him. He didn't deserve it. Ellie was right. And everyone knew it. That's why they were here tonight. Suzanna was so proud of her mother she could burst. She was able to divert her fury from Rutherford when she spotted Chase coming in the front door.

With a grateful smile, she pushed toward him. When they were close enough, he placed his hand on her arm. That one little gesture revealed more warmth and support than a thousand words could. "Anything happened yet?"

"The members are just arriving." She beamed at him. All his idea, huh? She definitely would have to thank him later. "Mama asked if you were coming. She wants to see you."

Chase scanned the crowd. "Where is she?"

"Probably in the center of the circle of reporters. They won't leave her alone for a minute."

"I'll find her. Got to give her a little good-luck kiss." He squeezed her hand before pushing through the crowd.

Suzanna checked the coffeepots and went after more sandwiches, trying to keep herself as busy as possible during the tense waiting.

The Rogues Club meeting lasted an hour, during which time gallons of coffee and hundreds of finger sandwiches were consumed. Finally the door opened and Alec descended, along with the club's officers.

In the glaring lights accompanying the television cameras, he read from a prepared statement. "The Rogues Club has evaluated the membership application of Ellie Schafer and, in an unprecedented vote, has elected her the first woman member of the club."

Cheers erupted from the local crowd.

While the president went on to list her "outstanding achievements in service to the community," the reporters were scrambling for their stories. And everyone began congratulating Ellie.

Suzanna joyously hugged her mother. "Hurray! You did it, Mama!" Then she stepped back so the others gathered around could give Ellie their personal congratulations.

Happier than she ever believed possible, Suzanna turned to face Rutherford. She smiled, ready to thank him, to receive his compliment, to say it was done at last.

His complexion was beet red. He reached for his cigar as he rumbled past her. "Hope you're satisfied, Suzanna."

Suddenly she realized that it wasn't over. It would never be over between them. He would never forget the incident and probably would blame her for her mother's actions. And Suzanna would always have to endure his chauvinistic attitude. She'd be willing to bet that he'd voted against her mother's membership.

In that emotion-packed moment, Suzanna knew exactly what she had to do in order to live with herself. "Mr. Rutherford, wait!"

He halted in the hallway but didn't turn.

She walked around in front of him. This was one time she wanted to look him in the eye. "I can see that you will never let me forget what my mother has done to your elite and biased Rogues Club. I won't deny that I support her wholeheartedly. Given the tremendous gaps between our philosophies and initiatives, I don't see how we can bridge them."

He shook his cigar at her. "Your mama hasn't helped matters any. I suspect that you put her up to all this."

Suzanna smiled, refusing to deny his accusations. He'd just clinched her suspicions. "There's an old country song that states exactly how I feel: 'Take This Job and Shove It.' And that's exactly what you can do with it, Mis-ter Rutherford."

He glared at her, not believing what she'd just said.

Suzanna wheeled around and headed for her office. She couldn't believe it, either. But she had never felt so sure—*and so absolutely, positively great!*—about a decision.

She stood in the middle of her office, her *ex-office*, taking deep breaths, reeling from the impact. Still not believing. Still not fully comprehending.

"Suzanna?"

She turned. It was Chase.

"Are you ready to go?" He studied her a moment and stepped inside. "What's wrong?"

"I just quit my job."

"You what?" He took another step toward her. "Why? What did Rutherford say to you?"

"Nothing much, actually. I just realized that this is not where I belong, working for him. You were right all along, Chase. He's a jerk, and I'm compromising my principles to play his petty, biased, sexist games."

Chase nodded slowly, accepting her explanation. He agreed with her, but this brought on other problems. "What'll you do?"

"I don't know yet. Maybe Ross and I will go to Little Rock. I'm sure I can find work in the city. There isn't much for me here in Grace."

"Suzanna, you can always work for me. The Boon Docks is growing. By spring, when we open up the float trips, we'll need someone to take charge and keep everything straight."

"Thanks, but—" she shook her head "—I don't think so. I wouldn't like that kind of relationship. Mixing business and private lives isn't a good idea."

"But what about us, Suz? What about our private lives?"

"I don't know, Chase. I haven't thought that far ahead."

"Do you think it's possible to retain what we have if you're in Little Rock?" He shook his head as if to answer his own question. "I'm asking you to stay. What would it take to keep you?"

"I need . . . I need more than a job from you Chase."

"Well, what? Suz, I'm afraid I can't give you what you really want."

How could he know? She hadn't even sorted it all out yet. "What's that, Chase?"

"Respectability, of course. You came back here to Grace looking for and trying to achieve respectability. You were determined to see that it happened. Remember? Only you got mixed up with me."

"Mixed up? Oh, Chase, you know I don't have any regrets about our relationship."

"Suzanna, I can't give you more. I'm me. Chase Clements, river rat. I'll never be anything more in this town."

"Where did you get this crazy idea about respectability?" She laughed a bit hysterically. "I don't give a damn about that, Chase. What I need most in our relationship is commitment. It's something I've never had."

"Surely you know that I . . . love you, Suz."

She blinked, visibly moved by his admission. He'd danced all around it during the many hours they'd spent together. But he'd never admitted his love until this moment. What a beautiful, difficult thing to say. She smiled through glistening tears, grateful to hear it at last. "I know. I love you, too, Chase. Guess I always have. And this sounds absolutely crazy, but love is not enough anymore. I'm sorry."

"Not enough? I've never said 'I love you' to *any* woman. And for you it isn't enough?"

She lifted her chin and stood her ground. "Darlene loves Ken, but there's no commitment. She can pick up and leave when it's convenient. She knows you'll take care of him.

"Zack loved us, in his own way. But he couldn't make a commitment, either. Ross and I always took care of ourselves. But now, before we launch into another relationship that steers our lives, we need stability. We need someone who'll share the love but will also be willing to make a long-term commitment to the responsibility. Apparently you aren't ready for that, either."

He glared at her, stunned by her statement, unable to give her a reply.

"Why don't you drop me off at the cottage on the way to picking up Ross? I have some packing to do."

They rode to the cottage in silence. When Chase brought Ross back, she half expected him to come in and talk. But he didn't. Then she knew why. He couldn't fulfill her needs. He couldn't give her the kind of commitment she needed. So, there was no need arguing about it. She understood. He was, after all, a river rat. And what did he know about commitment? Chase owed nothing to anybody. Not even to her.

Suzanna started packing that night. Why not? She couldn't sleep. A million times she asked herself why, oh, why she'd quit her job and turned down Chase's offer on the same night. She never did come up with an answer.

The next day, she and Ross were packing when Chase arrived with Ken.

The two Clements stood in the doorway of her living room, both grim-faced. Chase looked like hell. Apparently he'd been up half the night, too. He's probably been trying to figure out how to make this work, she thought. In her mind, there was only one way.

"Hi, Ken, Chase," Ross said with a resigned tone in his voice. He tossed something into the box. "We're moving again. I knew it was too good to last."

"Maybe not, Ross," Chase responded with a gentle smile for the boy. "If we can work things out. You see, Ken and I would like very much for y'all to stay in Grace."

"Are you going to help my mom find a good job?"

Chase looked at Suzanna. Although his eyes were red-rimmed, their expression seemed to caress her with love. "Better than that."

"Please, Chase," Suzanna began. "Don't make this more difficult." She looked at Ross and gestured. "Maybe you boys should go into the bedroom—"

"No!" Chase stepped forward. "They should stay. I want them to hear this. I have something important to say, something that directly affects them. And maybe you, too."

"I doubt it." She licked her lips and said tightly, "Chase, this is private and—"

"No, Suzanna, it isn't. This is a family affair. That's why I involved Ken in the decision. And why Ross should be a part of it, too. You see, I'm here to propose a lifelong commitment to both of you. That means marriage, because that's what folks do when they're in love. And I do love you, Suz, more than anything in this world. I think it's the time for us, don't you?"

"Chase, do you know what you're saying?" One hand went to her mouth, the other clutched her stomach. Suzanna felt as if she might be sick. Or might cry.

"I certainly do. I'm saying I love you so much that I'll do anything to keep you here, including marriage." He gestured at Ken. "We discussed this, and Ken agrees. I want you to be more than my friend. I want you to be my wife. Ken and I want to share our home and our lives and our love with you and with Ross."

The room went dead silent for a moment. Everyone gazed at Suzanna, waiting for an answer. She took a shaky breath and looked down at Ross who swallowed visibly, then asked, "Can we, Mom?"

"You, uh, want to?"

His answer was simple and to the point: "Yeah."

Suzanna glanced at Ken, who nodded affirmatively, agreeing with his father and Ross. And when she turned back to Chase, all she could do was hiccup ungracefully.

Chase frowned. "Suz, are you all right?" He moved forward and touched her arm.

At that tender gesture of his, following so closely his dramatic and entirely unexpected proposal, Suzanna did something very out-of-character: She started to cry.

Tears flooded her eyes. And they wouldn't stop. They rolled down her cheeks to make room for more. She blinked. "Oh, dear, I—" she sniffed "—can't believe—I'm doing this. . . ." She wiped her nose with her sleeve. "Oh, Chase . . ."

"My God, woman! Is that a yes, or what?"

"Yes." Her voice croaked and she repeated it more loudly. "Yes! *Yes!*"

Chase wrapped his arms around her waist, lifted her up and whirled her in a circle in the middle of the room. When he put her down, the boys joined in the merriment and hugged both her and Chase.

Finally, when they'd calmed down, Chase announced, "Hey, guys! We've got us a real family!"

Suzanna smiled happily at him, one of her arms around each boy. "It's what I've been holding out for, all along."

"What a great Christmas this is going to be!" Ross exclaimed, smiling at his mother. "Just when I thought we were hitting the road again."

"Oh, yes, it'll be a super Christmas!" Chase promised, tousling each boy's hair with a rough hand. "And I assure you the only time we're going to hit the road is on a family vacation to Disney World!"

"Disney World? Yeah!" Both boys jumped up and down excitedly. "When?"

"We'll decide later. Right now—" Chase took Suzanna in his arms and looked into her eyes "—excuse me, men. I need to show this lady my loving gratitude and everlasting affection. She's just agreed to marry me."

Ken and Ross giggled as Chase kissed Suzanna passionately. As the kiss continued, they groaned aloud and pretended to be bored. Finally, when the kiss seemed to go on forever, they shrugged and disappeared into Ross's room.

Meanwhile Suzanna and Chase vowed to continue the loving for a lifetime.

Back by Popular Demand

A romantic tour of America through fifty favorite Harlequin Presents, each set in a different state researched by Janet and her husband, Bill. A journey of a lifetime in one cherished collection.

In July, don't miss the exciting states featured in:

Title #11 — HAWAII
  Kona Winds

  #12 — IDAHO
  The Travelling Kind

Available wherever Harlequin books are sold.

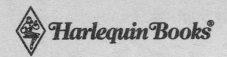
Harlequin Books®

GREAT NEWS . . .

HARLEQUIN UNVEILS NEW SHIPPING PLANS

For the convenience of customers, Harlequin has announced that Harlequin romances will now be available in stores at these convenient times each month*:

Harlequin Presents, American Romance, Historical, Intrigue:

> May titles: April 10
> June titles: May 8
> July titles: June 5
> August titles: July 10

Harlequin Romance, Superromance, Temptation, Regency Romance:

> May titles: April 24
> June titles: May 22
> July titles: June 19
> August titles: July 24

We hope this new schedule is convenient for you.

With only two trips each month to your local bookseller, you'll never miss any of your favorite authors!

*Please note: There may be slight variations in on-sale dates in your area due to differences in shipping and handling.

HDATES-RR

*Applicable to U.S. only.

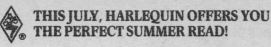
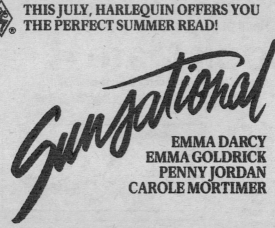